This book is dedicated to Mrs. P., who taught me how to read.

Sightings

1. Driver passes tall bipedal figure at night on Rawley Pike (Virginia)
2. Early evening sighting by a father and son of a bigfoot crossing interstate west of White Sulphur Springs (West Virginia)
3. Possible activity outside a home near Paw Paw (West Virginia)
4. Sightings by two hunters, one from a tree stand, outside Mingo (West Virginia)
5. Sighting by child outside her grandmother's home in Stumptown (West Virginia)
6. Homeowner reports interactions with his hunting dog near Prosperity (West Virginia)
7. Very close observation of a road crossing at night near Charmco (West Virginia)
8. 50 Acre Forest Fire in Boone County Believed to be Arson (West Virginia)
9. Home family reunion interrupted by visitor at the kitchen window near Hico (West Virginia)
10. Bigfoot spotted by driver in National Forest east of Camden-On-Gauley (West Virginia)
11. Youngster Sees Tall Creature near Wikel (West Virginia)
12. Pre-dawn sighting by a newspaper delivery man near Pickaway (West Virginia)
13. Nighttime encounter while training a coon hound outside Sinks Grove (West Virginia)
14. Husband and wife riding on an ATV spot a bigfoot near Becco (West Virginia)
15. The week in crime in Richwood, West Virginia from the Town Police Department crime report
16. Two sightings outside rural home near Decola (West Virginia)
17. Retired family doctor remembers daylight sighting as a teenager near Barboursville (West Virginia)
18. Witness sees a bipedal creature on a country road outside Horner (West Virginia)
19. 4:30 a.m. sighting by motorists on Ohio River Road outside Crown City (West Virginia)
20. Rare Albino Raccoon Spotted in a West Virginia Trash Bin; Seeing One is Less Likely Than Getting Hit by Lightning
21. Close rural community is on alert in Nettie (West Virginia)
22. Family group seen above visitors center on I-79 near Flatwoods (West Virginia)
23. Washington Post: Ersatz Sasquatch Has Feet of Clay, Police Say (Virginia)
24. ATV rider has a daylight encounter on his family farm near Wintergreen Resort (Virginia)
25. Runner shadowed by biped through heavy forest near Westlake Corner (Virginia)
26. Manlike figure seen in the trees by soldiers on guard duty at Radford Army Ammunition Plant (Virginia)
27. Driver sees large animal from the waist up along the roadside in Ararat (Virginia)
28. Sasquatch turns on homeowner after he orders his son to fire shotgun near Massanutten (Virginia)

Preface

This book did not start out as a book. It was a blog. Over time we found our readers truly loved our heartfelt posts. Several of them suggested we turn our writing into a book.

Here it is.

Along the way you will learn more about us than you could ever imagine. This is your chance to peek inside our heads during those few and precious moments when you spot one of us or we see one of you.

Driver passes tall bipedal figure at night on Rawley Pike (Virginia)

MISSION STATEMENT: My name is Barry. I am a Sasquatch. In late June my cousin Dave and I scared a couple of campers near Seneca Rocks, West Virginia. In their haste to leave, one of the campers dropped his smart phone and I found it. As long as the camper allows his phone account to remain active, my blog to explain bigfoot sightings will continue.

Update: The camper read my first post and has agreed to continue funding his smart phone. Thank you Camper One!

BIGFOOT SIGHTINGS EXPLAINED

Here is a report* from a driver who passed a tall bipedal figure on Rawley Pike in Virginia.

March 12, 2012, I was driving through the mountains of WV going east on Rawley Pike towards Virginia at 10 pm or so. I was out with my friend and I was driving. I took a turn and my headlights hit a figure walking along the road behind the guard rails. I'm 7 foot one but this thing was built, I'm tall but this must have been 6 inches to a foot taller than me. Though I was driving I was only going 15 mph around a turn so I had time to see it. It was walking behind the guard rail and there is no way it was a man, it was way too dark out. Right after I saw it I pretty much had a panic attack. My pulse went up and started breathing fast and shaking. I never believed there was such thing as one but I am sure I saw one. I just cannot believe how bad it scared me. My best friend was in the car and he claimed to see a black figure in the treeline he said "a larger than life black blur"

Here is the report* filed by an investigator after speaking to the eyewitness:

The witness is a very tall man, standing 7 feet 1 inch tall, and he describes himself as a bigfoot sceptic.
He was struck by the size of the creature he observed and knew that it was even taller than his own height, by several inches.
The figure was covered in black hair and walked quickly along behind the guard rail, as he passed by in his car.
It held its arms down to its sides while it moved and never turned to look at the witness' passing vehicle.

He describes the figures movement as odd, and unlike the manner in which a human would walk.

The witness drove with his windows down, and just before seeing the bipedal figure, he heard a vocalization that did not change pitch and lasted up to 6 seconds. It was so loud he initially believed he may have run over an animal.

The passenger did not get a good look and described what he saw as a "black blur as they passed".

The witness was immediately shaken by the observation and felt panicked. He was happy the figure did not turn to look at him as he's sure he would have lost control of his car.

The sighting took place along a stretch of Route 33 close to the Virginia/West Virginia state line.

The region is a rugged, forested and sparsely populated area of the George Washington National Forest.

This area has received reports over time on both sides of the state line.

Here is what really happened:

This sighting is a case of carelessness, pure and simple. Fred was walking along Rawley Pike (Rt. 33) on the evening of March 12, 2012. It's a pretty rugged climb all the way up to Wildcat Ridge and Fred is certifiably lazy. He'd rather stroll up the long and twisting blacktop road than trudge up the mountain through heavy brush.

Fred is almost eight feet tall, with hair as dark as a black cat. Moments before he heard the car's engine, Fred had been making whooping calls with the hope that his girlfriend was up on the ridge.

When he became aware of the car, Fred stepped off the road and crossed the guard rail. There was a very steep drop to his right and a fall would mean certain injury or death, so Fred kept his back to the headlights and continued walking. As the car passed, Fred caught a glimpse of two men inside the SUV. He got the impression they were college basketball players by the way they filled their seats.

Fred was pretty shaken up as well. He had violated the cardinal rule of our clan – TAKE ELUSIVE ACTION IF SPOTTED. At least the car continued up the mountain and Fred didn't have to dive off the cliff.

Fred feels really bad he freaked out the driver. He has since relocated to North Carolina.

*The BFRO.net website is the source for material used in this report. The report that appears here has been edited by Barry Bigfoot to conform with proper written English and the known facts.

SIGHTING TWO

Early evening sighting by a father and son of a bigfoot crossing interstate west of White Sulphur Springs (West Virginia)

MISSION STATEMENT: My name is Barry. I am a Sasquatch. In late June my cousin Dave and I scared a couple of campers near Seneca Rocks, West Virginia. In their haste to leave, one of the campers dropped his smart phone and I found it. As long as the camper allows his phone account to remain active, my blog to explain bigfoot sightings will continue.

Update: The camper read my first post and has agreed to continue funding his smart phone. Thank you Camper One!

BIGFOOT SIGHTINGS EXPLAINED

Here is a report* from a father and son who saw a bigfoot cross I-64 west of White Sulphur Springs, West Virginia.

While driving from Charlottesville, VA to Charleston, WV, on I-64, I saw what I assumed was a deer run into heavy east-bound traffic. One vehicle had to brake hard to avoid hitting this thing. When it came out between the cars and hit the grassy 70ft. median, it was running like a sprinter runs. I thought "That's not a deer, it's a man". He never slowed down when he got to the west-bound lanes and ran right behind a car passing an empty log truck. He almost ran into the rear of the truck, so he stopped. At this time I saw that he was covered from the top of his head to the ground with long dark brown hair. As soon as the truck passed, he sprinted across the lane and into the woods. The middle of his shoulder was even with the bottom of the cradle on the log trailer. When I passed this point, my 30 yr. old son saw him running up the hill through the woods.

Here is the report* filed by an investigator after speaking to the eyewitness:

When he initially saw the animal they were about 200 yards away, coming toward it. They were very close when the animal was forced to stop for the logging truck and he noted the hair color and length to be similar to an auburn colored golden retriever. They were close enough to see the hair "set down" when the creature stopped. Being able to compare the height of the animal to the logging truck, the father believed it was 6 – 6 1/2 feet tall.

I also talked to the 22 year old son who was in the passenger seat. He told me that he had heard of bigfoot before but did not know that they were in West Virginia. At the closest point he was about 50 feet from the animal as he was looking out the passenger window as the animal climbed the hill after crossing the interstate. He stated "I know what I saw and it was not a person".

Here is what really happened:

People just assume a Sasquatch is a big lumbering oaf. We do slow down gradually as we age but a juvenile bigfoot can outrun a world class Olympic sprinter.

On January 7, 2011, Zippy and Felicity were walking north through West Virginia's Greenbrier State Forest when they reached Interstate 64, a six lane divided highway. The sun had set to their left but Zippy did not want to wait until it was completely dark to cross the road. It turns out Zippy gets a sick thrill out of sprinting across traffic.

Without warning, Zippy lit out onto the Interstate and right into the path of a mini-van, which had to brake violently to avoid a collision. Zippy flew across the grassy median and raced into west bound traffic, straight into the path of a logging truck and a speeding car. He jogged in place as the truck passed, turned on the burners again and reached the other side of the highway in three jumps. He raced up to the tree line and waved to Felicity to come follow but she refused and Zippy had to cool his heels until nightfall before she crossed the highway.

Zippy is in his late teens, stands 6-1/2 feet tall and has long, light brown hair. He has an extensive history of anti-social behavior and one can only wonder what Felicity sees in him.

*The BFRO.net website is the source for material used in this report. The report that appears here has been edited by Barry Bigfoot to conform with proper written English and the known facts.

SIGHTING THREE

Possible activity outside a home near Paw Paw (West Virginia)

MISSION STATEMENT: My name is Barry. I am a Sasquatch. In late June my cousin Dave and I scared a couple of campers near Seneca Rocks, West Virginia. In their haste to leave, one of the campers dropped his smart phone and I found it. As long as the camper allows his phone account to remain active, my blog to explain bigfoot sightings will continue.

Update: The camper read my first post and has agreed to continue funding his smart phone. Thank you Camper One!

BIGFOOT SIGHTINGS EXPLAINED

Here is a report* from a homeowner who saw eye glow from three animals walking in single file outside his home.

3:00 am on October 11th, I got up out of bed to get a drink of water and was having trouble falling asleep. As I walked by my kitchen window, I peered out and noticed three pairs of red eyes walking single file about 20 yards up in the woods. I've been a hunter and outdoorsman since I was 6 yrs old and have seen many animals and eyes at night so I wasn't all that surprised. But what really had me perplexed was the height at which the eyes were above ground level. I would estimate that the eyes were hovering around the 7 ft mark at least so that rules out any wildlife that I'm familiar with. The intensity of the glowing red was also unlike anything I have ever experienced or seen before and the creatures appeared to be walking with comfortable balance and agility. It was pitch black and could not make out any silhouettes except a few branches moving. There is 4 miles worth of wilderness behind my house and most of it is government land. I have no idea what I saw that night but am open minded to it being a sasquatch or another creature that I'm unfamiliar with. Have not talked much about it to other people and am afraid people will think I'm losing it but I can't stop thinking about what I saw.

About a week prior to this event, I was awakened in the middle of the night by what sounded like a baseball bat or pipe being whacked off of a tree and then something like metal being smashed. I found that to be very bizarre. Especially it was going on around 3am in the morning.

Here is the report* filed by an investigator after speaking to the eyewitness:

This witness and I talked for about 45 minutes about his sighting and I found him to be a kind and amiable man.

Speaking to the gentleman over the phone, he said that he observed three pairs of eyes moving laterally behind his house and into the woods. He also said that he is a long time coon hunter and has never seen any eye shine in the woods at night like this. The eyes appeared to be as red as a coke bottle's cap, but larger. He did not notice any "bounce" in the eyes, so whatever it was moved in a smooth gait. There is steep terrain and thick cover where they entered the woods, but whatever it was seemed to move quickly and easily.

The following morning he walked to the location where he saw the eyes disappear into the woods and found a fresh tree branch break approximately 4-5″ in diameter. He didn't think to look for tracks, but the ground cover did not lend well to showing footprints. He also struggled to climb to where he lost sight of them, even though whatever it was managed the terrain easily the previous night. His neighbor's dogs had began barking at approximately 11:30 PM and had continued for an hour or so and this seemed very strange to him. He had also heard knocks approximately five minutes apart a few weeks prior to this incident.

Here is what really happened:

Those three sets of eyes moving across the yard in single file belonged to Larry, Moe and Curly. Each is over seven feet tall. Before they were born, their mother loved to stand in the woods behind the Bengies Drive-In Theatre and watch Three Stooges movies. That's why she chose those names for her boys. How appropriate.

The stooges do everything as a team and they do it badly. Whenever they enter unfamiliar territory, instead of taking cover and doing reconnaissance, they march in formation like fat geese. And they think it's funny to scare house pets by banging metal trash cans and smashing tree limbs. I don't know how they've made it this far. If it were not for frogs and road kill, they would starve.

*The BFRO.net website is the source for material used in this report. The report that appears here has been edited by Barry Bigfoot to conform with proper written English and the known facts.

SIGHTING FOUR

Sightings by two hunters, one from a tree stand, outside Mingo (West Virginia)

MISSION STATEMENT: My name is Barry. I am a Sasquatch. In late June my cousin Dave and I scared a couple of campers near Seneca Rocks, West Virginia. In their haste to leave, one of the campers dropped his smart phone and I found it. As long as the camper allows his phone account to remain active, my blog to explain bigfoot sightings will continue.

Update: The camper read my first post and has agreed to continue funding his smart phone. Thank you Camper One!

BIGFOOT SIGHTINGS EXPLAINED

Here is a report* from two hunters who separately encountered the same bigfoot:

It happened on a hunting trip in West Virginia. We were on our yearly deer-hunting trip in the remote mountainous. I was about 26 years old and was in on leave from the military on the family-hunting trip. My family and friends have hunted this area for many years and I was very comfortable and familiar with the area.

The light had just begun to peek over the mountaintop when I cleared my spot and settled in. I had worked up a pretty good sweat on the steady pace up the mountain so it was not too long after setting and listening to the first morning light waking up the rest of the forest, I began to nod off to sleep. After going in and out a few times, I decided to get up and move around a little to try to wake myself up.

After about 20 minutes of walking around I stumbled on a very old wooden tree stand. Although I could tell it had been there for many years, I remember thinking it was in the best spot overlooking the very visible and open woods just under the crest of the hilltop.

Not too long after I ate the apples and oranges I had brought. After a while the warm morning sun took its toll on me and I nodded off again.

A bad smell woke me right up. The forest was completely quiet around me and all I could think of is what the hell that awful smell is? As I became more alert, I could hear the slight rustling below me and what I thought was some faint grunts and whines. I decided it was time to lean over and get a visual on it.

It was about 25 feet below me on the slope and directly in front of the stand. It was not aware of my presence above it. It was about 5 feet tall with long dark, reddish-brown hair. The hair from its head down its body was of equal length, about 2-3 inches long. The hair went down its arms and hands as well as its feet. I could barley see fingernails and toe nails. Not claws but nails like a human.

Most of its hair was tangled and matted in spots as if it had wallowed the ground or a tree or something. I watched it smelling the orange peels and apple core then tasting them. It looked around at one point as if to wonder where they may have come from. I wondered how long it would be before it became aware of my presence and what it would do when it did.

Then I heard the rustling coming down from the top of the hill, loud rustling, and I could tell something was coming at a pretty rapid speed. I saw the one below me turn and look in the direction of the noise. It froze for a few seconds and looked almost like a statue.

I could not see at this point what was coming down the hill. I was leaning to my right and looking down. I tried to move my eyes to the left but my view was blocked by the trees that was holding up my stand and partially by the full-brim hat I was wearing. I kept my eyes moving between the one below me and the direction of the disturbance coming down the hill.

As it moved toward our position it began to make noises like I have never heard before. I would ordinarily not be able to describe the noise but I have read where other people have described it as a record being played backward. I would have to say that is a very close description. It is as if it were speaking a language but nothing like I have ever heard before.

The one below me sprang to its feet and then moved about 15-20 feet to the right of me. It moved very rapidly, kind of between a run and a leap, all on its feet though. It did not use its arms. It then started to bellow back at the one coming down the hill and it sounded almost like they were arguing. That is the impression that it left me with anyway.

It wasn't until the one above me came into clear view that I started to feeling very scared. As it came into my immediate area it moved toward the first one and began to slow to what seemed to be very cautious movements. Its attention seemed to move between the first creature and its surrounding area. I felt at this moment that it was alert to my presence.

This second one was much larger than the first and it seemed very irritated. The bigger one was covered in very dark hair, almost black. It was very muscular and its arms were noticeably long. It stood with a slight bend but an upright posture. I had to be about 8-9 feet tall. It was much larger than a human.

As these two creatures squabbled (communicated?) back and forth their gestures were extremely human-like. I was under the impression that the larger of the two was scolding the smaller one.

They moved about 40-50 feet to the right of me. At this point the larger one had its back to me I could make out facial features of the smaller one. It had very human-like features but a different nose. Hair covered most of its face but it looked to be thin hair, not like the rest of it.

Then the smaller creature spotted me because it went into a crouched and then squatting position and looked up in my direction. Their chattering began to quiet and then the larger one, with its back still to me, went into a squatting position for a few seconds. The smaller one then began to howl and bellow very loudly. The larger of the one, with its back still toward me began to howl very loud also. The larger creature then pushed the smaller one and the smaller one sprang to its feet and rapidly ran off across the hill to my right. It ran in long leaping strides and moved very fast like nothing I had ever seen. I never noticed it to ever look back.

As the smaller one ran the larger one stood up and slowly turned toward me. It had its arm bent above its forehead as if it were shading or hiding its eyes. It stood very straight and tall and looked directly at my tree stand.

All of the fear from before overcame me again and I prayed that thing did not try to come up my tree. I thought for an instant that I would yell at it, jerk or jump and maybe frighten it away but I could not bring myself to move. I could not even bat an eye. I could feel my legs starting to shake and I became very hot all over. For an instant I though I was going to pass out or become physically ill.

For a brief moment it was looking right at my face. From what I could see it had very large human-like eyes and very large round nostrils. I could not make out lips because of the hair on its face but I would guess that they were thin lips because the hair did not stick out. It did not have much of a protruding mouth or jaw like an ape. It had a flat fairly face like a human.

It put its arm to its side and began to look around. It swiveled at the hips and looked in every direction. After a quick glance back at me it then began to walk off in the direction the smaller one had gone. It did not run or act scared at all. It made very long howls as it walked and turned a few times and looked in my direction as it walked away.

I watched it and listened until it became just a black figure moving through the woods. I could here it howl and bellow for a few more minutes. Then I heard what sounded like something beating a tree or log with a limb or stick or something.

After about 30 minutes I decided that if it meant to do me harm, it sure had the chance, and it was probably safe to get down out of the tree stand. I made my way back toward my friend that I had left earlier that morning. As I walked closer to him I asked him if he had seen anything. He was very pale and I could tell he was a little scared and puzzled and then he answered to me the he was not sure what he had saw.

I said, "You look like you saw a Bigfoot!" and he jumped to his feet and asked, "Did you see it?"

I nodded to him, yes, then he began to tell me what he saw. Apparently the larger creature had moved across the hill in front of him crashing through the trees about 40 to 50 yards away. He said at first he thought it was a bear but after observing it, he could plainly see that it was moving very fast and walking upright, like a man.

This really happened. I have never returned to that area of the woods.

Here is the report* filed by an investigator after speaking to the eyewitness:

I spoke with the witness about the incident and about himself. He is credible and I believe he accurately described what he observed that day.

Here is what really happened:

Everyone in the woods knows it – you don't want to ever find yourself standing between a female bear and one of her cubs. The same thing holds true here, but in this instance, our witness was stuck up a tree stand between Mrs. B and her seven year old son Timmy. Mrs. B still remembers the incident. She had left Timmy to poke around for insects while she walked over the hill to do some reconnaissance. That's when she spotted the hunter's friend.

"That same freakin' family of hunters is back!" she shrieked as she spun around and raced back to Timmy. The hunter's friend saw Mrs. B as she crashed through the brush.

As she's running, Mrs. B keeps shrieking, "Stay in one place, Timmy. Don't you go nowhere, Timmy. Don't make me have to say this more than twice!"

She was quick to place herself between the hunter and her son. Then she said to Timmy,

"Listen to me, you little fool. Look up in those trees. Up there, behind me, over my left shoulder," she pointed.

"Where?" said Timmy.

"Up there, about 25 feet. What do you see?"

"Holy crap! Is that a hunter?"

"Yes, it's a hunter!"

"What's he doing there? Is he going to shoot us?"

"He's not going to shoot anybody. The only thing he's gonna do is poop his pants. My back is turned to him, so when I give you a little push, get up and run as fast as you can over the next hill and wait for me there. I'll deal with the hunter."

She nudged her son and he bolted to the right and went over the hill.

Mrs. B turned around and faced the hunter. She raised her arm to shield the light of the morning sun and fixed him square in the eyes with a glare that said,

"I see you mother 'effer and if you were a stupid deer I would snap your neck with one hand."

Then she lowered her arm, made a 360 degree scan of the perimeter and started walking towards Timmy.

She kept peeking back at the hunter and growling, "Every year that family has to come back here and spoil everything. A body can't count on peace and quiet in a national forest any more. And Timmy, he's eating apple cores off the ground and not thinking about how they got there. He didn't get that from me!"

*The BFRO.net website is the source for material used in this report. The report that appears here has been edited by Barry Bigfoot to conform with proper written English and the known facts.

SIGHTING FIVE

Sighting by child outside her grandmother's home in Stumptown (West Virginia)

MISSION STATEMENT: My name is Barry. I am a Sasquatch. In late June my cousin Dave and I scared a couple of campers near Seneca Rocks, West Virginia. In their haste to leave, one of the campers dropped his smart phone and I found it. As long as the camper allows his phone account to remain active, my blog to explain bigfoot sightings will continue.

Update: The camper read my first post and has agreed to continue funding his smart phone. Thank you Camper One!

BIGFOOT SIGHTINGS EXPLAINED

Here is a report* made by the parent of a child who had a surprise encounter:

My grandmother went to my aunt's house in Alabama for a month, so my wife and I said we would feed her dog and check on her house while she was away. we only live about 3/4 a mile from her house. my wife and daughter went over to feed the dog. my wife was on the back porch. my daughter ran around the house after the dog. as soon as she got out of sight my wife heard her scream and come running back. my wife heard something going through the brush. my wife asked her what happened. my daughter said a monkey growled at her and ran into the woods. later she said it was a little one with its mom. I don't know what it was but my daughter was really scared. we live in a wooded area. she sees bears and a lot of other animals and she said it looked like a monkey.

Here is the report* filed by an investigator after speaking to the eyewitness:

Talked to the witnesses' father about his daughter's sighting. We discussed other things happening in the area which puzzled him. He has cut several trees from a riding trail which nobody else uses. The trees are pushed over in such a location that its impossible for a horse to walk around them. I asked about deadfall which would accompany windstorms around the downed trees. He reported that there was very few smaller limbs near the road blocks. He has heard unusual cries and screams, not at all like bobcats or mountain lions with which he is familiar.

The child entered a computer room while her father was looking at the BFRO website. She noticed the screen and remarked, "That's the monkey I saw!"

Here is what really happened:

The young witness appears to be very well adjusted after such a traumatic experience. Two times, using only her limited knowledge of the world, the little girl said she saw a monkey.

What she actually saw was Mrs. T with her baby daughter. Only the day before, Mrs. T had watched the grandmother leave the property with her camper. Mrs. T was looking forward to some peace and quiet for a couple of weeks.

But no, from around the corner, here comes sweet little Suzie.

"Beat it!" Mrs. T growled at the little girl, then picked up her daughter and dashed into the brush.

Mrs. T is a parent, too. She was concerned the incident might have inflicted some psychological damage on little Suzie. She's pleased the girl had the wisdom to say she saw a monkey. That description is not complementary to us (monkeys are below you guys on the evolutionary tree) but the description works for an innocent child.

Mrs. T hopes Suzie grows up to be the next Jane Goodall.

*The BFRO.net website is the source for material used in this report. The report that appears here has been edited by Barry Bigfoot to conform with proper written English and the known facts.

SIGHTING SIX

Homeowner reports interactions with his hunting dog near Prosperity (West Virginia)

MISSION STATEMENT: My name is Barry. I am a Sasquatch. In late June my cousin Dave and I scared a couple of campers near Seneca Rocks, West Virginia. In their haste to leave, one of the campers dropped his smart phone and I found it. As long as the camper allows his phone account to remain active, my blog to explain bigfoot sightings will continue.

Update: The camper read my first post and has agreed to continue funding his smart phone. Thank you Camper One!

BIGFOOT SIGHTINGS EXPLAINED

Here is a report* from a homeowner about his hunting dog:

A week ago my dog was making a strange noise like he was playing, but it was around midnight. I called my friend who lives on the property to meet me. We went up the hill to my dog pen and my dog was acting as if he was playing, all happy, running around and looking behind him.

We shined our lights up the hill and saw a rather large figure, about seven to eight feet tall and rather thick, step back into the darkness and disappear. It scared us and we ran. We have been hearing sounds every night. Last night we went out around 1:00 AM. Something growled back, not like a bear, and was very close and kept following us.

My dog is still doing the same thing every night and my cats refuse to stay out at night. Before this started, they wouldn't come in.

We live on the side of a mountain with about two thousand hunting lease acres behind us and neighbors about a third of a mile away. We are on a dead end road with lots of animals and very secluded. Deer would walk around in our yard on most days before this started and we regularly see bears up here.

Here is the report* filed by an investigator after speaking to the eyewitness:

I spoke to the witness in mid-December. He added details that occurred in the time since he filed the report.

He and his friend (who lives in a cabin on the witness' property) have seen a figure walking on the ridge top several times since the original incident.

They have had rocks thrown at their respective dwellings, each thinking the other was creating a prank. Calling each other on the cell phone, they discovered they were both inside while rocks hit each building simultaneously. Possibly, there is more than one rock thrower.

He reported screams at night, angry growls following the witness and additional incidents with his hunting dogs. The midnight visitor seems curious about his animals, having not attempted to harm any of them.

Here is what really happened:

For every one hundred dogs who lose it completely when they hear or smell a Sasquatch, there's always one dog who really loves us. This hunting dog was overjoyed with his nightly visits from Lonesome Bob, a bulky eight-footer who is a natural with domestic animals, even troublesome ones. Bob could quiet a yapping Chihuahua if he had to, especially if it meant a successful raid on a vegetable garden or a rabbit hutch.

He was kind to pets, there is no doubt about that, but Bob and his pal Bosco spent a lot of evenings punking the homeowner and his tenant friend. The usual stuff — shrieking, howling, growling, rock tossing, branch snapping – unexpected noises that send a frightened homeowner racing out in his pajamas in the dark of the night wondering what the hell is going on. Bob and Bosco would watch from the ridge top and bust a gut laughing.

Innocent stuff but pretty annoying at the same time.

*The BFRO.net website is the source for material used in this report. The report that appears here has been edited by Barry Bigfoot to conform with proper written English and the known facts.

SIGHTING SEVEN

Very close observation of a road crossing at night near Charmco (West Virginia)

MISSION STATEMENT: My name is Barry. I am a Sasquatch. In late June my cousin Dave and I scared a couple of campers near Seneca Rocks, West Virginia. In their haste to leave, one of the campers dropped his smart phone and I found it. As long as the camper allows his phone account to remain active, my blog to explain bigfoot sightings will continue.

Update: The camper read my first post and has agreed to continue funding his smart phone. Thank you Camper One!

BIGFOOT SIGHTINGS EXPLAINED

Here is a report* from a driver who saw a bigfoot from 30 feet:

On my way home this evening at 8 pm, I was driving down the mountain when I saw what I thought was a bear. I slowed down, just in case it ran out in front of me, when it stepped over the guard rail, I knew it wasn't a bear. I rolled my window up. it turned, looked at me. I had my bright lights on. In two steps it crossed the two lane road, then went up the mountain. Scared, omg, can't believe what I saw, still shook up! Very dark, that animal was dark, matted hair, from what I could see in my headlights. My guess, height wise, close to nine foot. Very tall. Happened near Charmco, West Virginia.

Here is the report* filed by an investigator after speaking to the eyewitness:

I talked to this witness at length about her sighting that happened on her way to work. In addition to what she put in the original report, I can add the following greater details from our conversation.

While driving down the mountain at about 40 mph she saw a deer jump the guardrail and run across the road looking back across the road. She slowed to almost a stop anticipating another deer to cross as well. The Bigfoot stepped over the guardrail about 30 feet in front of her and looked at her stopped vehicle. She started honking her horn and flashing her lights to try to scare it. She was shaking as soon as she saw the animal. It turned and in two steps crosses the road and goes into the woods.

She noticed the dark reddish-brown hair, large eyes which reflected an orangish color. She was struck by the enormous size. Her brother is 6′ 7″ and a big guy but would be dwarfed by the size of this animal.

The animal in no way seemed aggressive.

The nearest house was about a mile away

She has seen all types of wildlife on that road including bears and she is adamant that she knows what she saw.

When she got to work she told the other workers what she had seen. She was later approached by a woman whose father is a coal miner and had apparently seen a Bigfoot in the middle of the night close to the same location about two years prior.

She gets very nervous and anxious when thinking about the sighting. Now before going to bed at night she makes sure her outside lights are on and all her dogs are inside.

It is very remote with a lot of terrain, similar to almost everywhere in West Virginia.

Here is what really happened:

This report sounds like one of those split-second roadside sightings — an unsuspecting driver sees a strange animal and watches it disappear — but there's a whole lot more here than that.

A. Let's look at the time line. How many seconds did it take the witness to:

1. see a deer run across the road while it was looking back. 2. spot the bigfoot on her right and think it was a bear. 3. know it was not a bear. 4. watch it lift it's leg and step over the guard rail onto the road, 5. slow her car from 40 mph to a complete stop. 6. roll up her window. 7. sit in panic while the bigfoot "looked at her stopped vehicle". 7. take note of it's dark reddish brown matted hair and it's large eyes which reflected an orangish color. 8. compare it's massive height to her brother, who is 6'7". 9. honk her horn. 10. flash her lights. 11. watch the bigfoot turn. 12. see it cross the road and enter the woods?

My guess: 25 seconds.

B. Here is who the witness saw:

Gene is a Peeping Tom, but hey, we all are. Gene watches a lot of television, especially when homeowners fall asleep with the TV still playing in the bedroom. Gene really loves "Dancing With The Stars". A Sasquatch will nervously rock back and forth while he's peeking, so Gene has worked up a lot of terrific dance moves.

Friends have seen Gene late at night, in the midst of a driving thunderstorm, acting out that famous scene from "Singing in the Rain," splashing in puddles and holding on with one hand as he dances around the light pole at the Quickie Mart.

On the evening in question, Gene was stalking a doe when he saw the witnesses' car in the distance. To Gene, those headlights were a spotlight. He couldn't help himself.

C. Here is what the witness missed in her confusion:

Gene could not wait to hop over the rail and step into the light. The car stopped with him smack in the middle of the road.

Gene started his set with a moon walk a la Michael Jackson, spun around in a pirouette, twisted and turned like Elvis Presley, dropped into a leg split like James Brown and danced off stage like Fred Astaire.

He thought his moves rated a high score. He's sorry the witness completely missed the audition while she was in shock.

He is saddened to hear that she's still anxious about the sighting and keeps her dogs inside and her lights on.

He hopes his heartfelt explanation will lessen her fears but he doubts it will, mostly because he's nine feet tall and he took her by complete surprise. Gene will not be bothering the witness again. He's moved to Hudson Valley, New York and is monitoring dinner theater productions of Cats, Oklahoma and West Side Story.

*The BFRO.net website is the source for material used in this report. The report that appears here has been edited by Barry Bigfoot to conform with proper written English and the known facts.

SIGHTING EIGHT

50 Acre Forest Fire in Boone County Believed to be Arson (West Virginia)

MISSION STATEMENT: My name is Barry. I am a Sasquatch. In late June my cousin Dave and I scared a couple of campers near Seneca Rocks, West Virginia. In their haste to leave, one of the campers dropped his smart phone and I found it. As long as the camper allows his phone account to remain active, my blog to explain bigfoot sightings will continue.

Update: The camper read my first post and has agreed to continue funding his smart phone. Thank you Camper One!

BIGFOOT SIGHTINGS EXPLAINED

Here is a news release from the Boone County Times:

BOONE COUNTY, W.Va. — Fire crews have contained an overnight forest fire in Boone County that spanned about 50 acres in the Dartmont area.

John Bindernagel with the West Virginia Division of Forestry says fire crews were on the scene Monday night and returned Tuesday morning to help contain the blaze.

Crews believe the fire was arson.

According to forestry officials, arson fires are uncommon in the Dartmont and Ashford areas.

Investigators say they are pursuing leads in the case and are offering a reward for anyone with any information.

According to forestry officials, two individuals who reserved a camping site at the location where the fire started have been detained and are being questioned.

Here is what really happened:

Stevie found a dead possum on the side of Route 18 and he was delighted with his find. Just by chance he'd found a disposable lighter earlier in the day and the lighter still had a couple of flicks of life left in it.

Stevie stepped into the woods and headed for a secluded campsite with a fire pit.

Stevie had watched from a safe distance as lots of folks started camp fires, so monkey see – monkey do, he gathered some dry twigs and brush, flicked the Bic and a short time later he was enjoying charred road kill, with roasted carrots stolen from a vegetable garden and a warm twelve pack of Bud Lights he'd lifted from the bed of a pick-up truck.

Stevie fell asleep and the fire quickly torched 50 acres of prime forest.

I e-mailed a copy of this blog to the attorney who is representing the campers who were detained by forestry officials and another copy to the sheriff of Boone County. Little good that will do. Try telling a judge the fire was started by a bigfoot using a disposable lighter. That has be worse than saying the dog ate my homework. And officially, we don't exist anyway.

<h3 style="text-align:center">SIGHTING NINE</h3>

Home family reunion interrupted by visitor at the kitchen window near Hico (West Virginia)

MISSION STATEMENT: My name is Barry. I am a Sasquatch. In late June my cousin Dave and I scared a couple of campers near Seneca Rocks, West Virginia. In their haste to leave, one of the campers dropped his smart phone and I found it. As long as the camper allows his phone account to remain active, my blog to explain bigfoot sightings will continue.

Update: The camper read my first post and has agreed to continue funding his smart phone. Thank you Camper One!

<h3 style="text-align:center">BIGFOOT SIGHTINGS EXPLAINED</h3>

Here is a report* from a witness who remembers a family gathering interrupted by a visitor at the kitchen window.

We visited my dad's family during the summer break. I noticed my grandmother kept looking over her right shoulder towards the large kitchen window. She suddenly grabbed my grandfather's leg and whispered "There's something in that window!"

My grandfather looked at the window and calmly went into his bedroom. He called my father and my three uncles and asked them to come after him.

I got up and went in also as my granddad was taking guns off the rack and he said, "There is something at that back window. We got to run it off." My dad and his brothers smiled at each other, thinking it was a joke until granddad loaded his double barrel 12 gauge (granddad did NOT play with guns).

My dad and my uncles took the guns and ammo and started for the front door. I being the oldest grandson tagged along at the rear (with an unloaded .22 rifle) feeling like I was one of the men. I remember feeling scared but also brave going out in the dark to deal with this bear or whatever it was.

Granddad and one uncle got to the rear of the house, turned the corner and froze in their tracks. My uncle said "Daddy what the hell?" My granddad fired both barrels one after the other. I dropped my gun, spun around and headed back to the front door, which was locked tight!

I was pounding on the door and screaming, "Let me in!" I looked to my left and where the roof meets the wall of the house I saw the outline of one shoulder and a head and two small greenish yellow eyes reflected in the porch light.

During this time the men were at the rear of the house, the women and kids were inside screaming because of the shotgun blasts and I was pounding on the front door all, within about 5 seconds of the shots.

My dad came around from the right side looking for me. I pointed to what I saw and he put me behind him, yelling for them to open the door. In about 3 seconds we were all back in the house and pretty well freaked out.

None of us slept well that night. I do remember my granddad talking to himself saying, "Wonder where them dogs got off to?"

A couple years later, I asked my granddad what is was he saw that night and he said it was not a bear, that's for sure. By the way, the kitchen window is about 8 feet off the ground due to the slope of the mountain.

Four dogs which stay around the house at night were gone during the sighting but came back scared in the morning, so scared that they pushed their way into the house. These dogs had never seen the inside of a house before that morning.

OTHER WITNESSES: dad and one uncle saw the shape and size in the dark, two uncles saw just head, face and eyes in low light

Here is the report* filed by an investigator after speaking to the eyewitness:

Witness stated that following this incident, his grandmother made a change in her walking habits. Previously she carried a .22 rifle when walking in the woods. Following that night, she switched to carrying a Winchester 30-30 on her daily walk.

There were no more visitations following the events of this night. His grandfather told him of an unseen individual throwing rocks at him while camping in another location in the same county.

Here is what really happened:

Serious guns, serious grandpa.

The kid said, "My grandad fired both barrels, one after the other" but the question remains, what happened after he fired the rifle?

Here is what the dad and the three uncles saw:

The dad and one of the uncles saw the shape and size in the dark. The other two uncles saw head, face and eyes in low light.

The kid saw something so terribly frightening he dropped his rifle and bolted.

What each one of them saw was Earl, an eight-footer who only moments before had been standing at the kitchen window and was now beating a path out of the yard. When the kid ran around the house, he stumbled upon Monroe, who was cowering on the front porch.

Earl says it is lucky for him the old man can't hit the broad side of a barn, even from close up, and neither can his paranoid wife. They're both blind as bats. He thinks they shouldn't be living out in the country by themselves anymore.

Earl likes to spook the old lady when she's taking her walks and can't resist peeking at her through the kitchen window to freak her out even more, but on that night grandpa had had enough of her panic attacks. His whole family was there. He was the head of the household. He had to do something.

And his shotgun blasts? Grandpa missed Earl by the length of a truck and nearly killed the neighbor's cow.

Earl and Monroe left the property for good after that. They can take a hint.

The old lady, she still might hit something with that big gun. At the sound of a cricket, she'll spin around and blast away.

Oh yeah, the rock throwing incident at another location? Earl was up on a ridge and spotted grandpa down below. He grunted to Monroe, "There's that Doofus who shot at me" and started heaving boulders at the old man before Monroe pulled him away.

*The BFRO.net website is the source for material used in this report. The report that appears here has been edited by Barry Bigfoot to conform with proper written English and the known facts.

Bigfoot spotted by driver in National Forest east of Camden-On-Gauley (West Virginia)

MISSION STATEMENT: My name is Barry. I am a Sasquatch. In late June my cousin Dave and I scared a couple of campers near Seneca Rocks, West Virginia. In their haste to leave, one of the campers dropped his smart phone and I found it. As long as the camper allows his phone account to remain active, my blog to explain bigfoot sightings will continue.

Update: The camper read my first post and has agreed to continue funding his smart phone. Thank you Camper One!

BIGFOOT SIGHTINGS EXPLAINED

Here is a report* from a driver who spotted a bigfoot in the middle of the road in the middle of a National Forest.

I left a camp ground and took a short cut that comes out in Camden on Gauley to get home. It was midnight (12:03 to be exact.) I was almost to the county line when I saw what I thought at first was some idiot in a monkey suit in the middle of the road in front of me. I beeped my horn at it. He started to run very fast, in long strides and then I realized it wasn't a man. He wasn't wearing shoes. His feet looked hairy. He was covered in reddish brown hair and about six feet tall. The hair was all even in length. He ran about quarter of a mile up the hill in front of me then tore through some elderberry bushes and disappeared down the mountain. I only got a really quick glimpse of his face so I can't accurately describe it. The next day I went back and looked at the spot where he ran through the bushes. There were some kind of prints in the mud holes in the road and the elderberry bushes were broken and bent where it went through. I took a friend up there the next day to show her where it happened. She and I looked at the prints. She spends a lot of time in the woods and thought the print in the mud looked like a big heel print.

When I told my grandma about it, she said that area was notorious for what we call Yahoos (pronounced yay-hoo because that's the sound people have heard them make). In fact, that hollow was called Yahoo Hollow by her age group. Another family member said he treed something strange up there about fifty years earlier and my grandma's teacher told the story of how one was on her porch one day. Grandma said her teacher described it just the same as what I saw except it had dark brown hair and was about seven foot tall.

Here is the report* filed by an investigator after speaking to the eyewitness:

I spoke to this witness at length.

He still has a vivid memory of that night. He has grown up in the mountains which have many bears and he is sure that he did not see a bear.

He took his grandmother out where the incident happened and she told him that the area was called "Yayhoo Holler". "Yayhoo" is a common name for bigfoot in the mountain regions of West Virginia.

When the creature turned to look at him, he saw that it had a "flattish, ape-like face". The hair on the body of the creature was similar to an orangutan's hair.

The area of the sighting is in the Monongahela National Forest, which is a remote million acre tract in West Virginia.

Here is what really happened:

The driver sees an idiot in a monkey suit standing in the road in the middle of nowhere at three minutes after midnight. He honks his horn. The idiot takes off running, straight up the hill for a quarter of a mile before crashing through some bushes and disappearing down the mountain.

It ran on two legs, with long strides and it went very fast. The driver then decided it wasn't a man in a monkey suit. No shoes. Hairy feet. Covered in reddish brown hair. Six feet. Flattish, ape-like face. After the quarter mile, it tore through bushes and left heel prints. The region has a history of sightings. The natives call this thing a Yayhoo.

Francis is the idiot in the monkey suit. He is in his middle teens. He stands over six feet tall and has reddish brown hair. Francis has a runner's mentality. When you are the best at something in your community or age group (Francis is a two-time Southern Regional Junior Champion at the quarter mile), you have to find ways to test yourself.

Automobiles rarely roll through the Cranberry region of the Monongahela National Forest at night. Francis will wait at his starting block for hours, stretching, breaking off and stopping, warming up over and over until he sees headlights in the distance.

A car rolls up and Francis rolls out. In most cases, the witness is so terrified she will race Francis nose-to-nose for the quarter mile and even farther.

In this case, the driver honked his horn and Francis interpreted that honk as a signal to GO! The witness watched in amazement as an idiot in a monkey suit set a new land-speed record for the quarter mile while running up hill.

Francis thinks his behavior is in keeping with our cardinal rule, TAKE ELUSIVE ACTION IF SPOTTED, but there's no doubt he's stretching things here.

Yayhoo? What kind of name is that? Personally, it's no worse than Bigfoot, Yetti, Skunk Ape, Abominable Snowman or Sasquatch. You say tomato, I say tomatoe.

SIGHTING ELEVEN

Youngster Sees Tall Creature near Wikel (West Virginia)

MISSION STATEMENT: My name is Barry. I am a Sasquatch. In late June my cousin Dave and I scared a couple of campers near Seneca Rocks, West Virginia. In their haste to leave, one of the campers dropped his smart phone and I found it. As long as the camper allows his phone account to remain active, my blog to explain bigfoot sightings will continue.

Update: The camper read my first post and has agreed to continue funding his smart phone. Thank you Camper One!

BIGFOOT SIGHTINGS EXPLAINED

Here is a report* from a 12-year old female:

On the morning of July 4, I think I had an experience with a Sasquatch. I was walking up the driveway to the house just after getting the mornings newspaper.

Because it happened to be very hot during the day, I put the newspaper down to put my hair up. When I looked up after putting my hair up, I saw a big, tanish brown creature that had a sort of hump in its back. Its fur was short and clumped together.

It then ran off into the woods. I was frightened, so I ran back to the house. Once inside I heard banging on the trees in the yard. These bangings have been occurring quite frequently now. I've also noticed that wildlife activity in the area is low.

Poundings (wood knocking) were heard in the area shortly after the incident.

Here is the report* filed by an investigator after speaking to the eyewitness:

The 12 year old witness showed me the exact spot where she observed the creature and talked me through its movements following discovery. She was about ¼ mile from the family home down a long driveway and observed it moving from one tree line to another. She said when the creature noticed her; it turned in her direction and took several steps toward her. Thereupon she ran back home yelling for her mother and sister.

Her mother stated that B. is not easy to scare and upon seeing her face, asked what happened. It was obvious something was very wrong as she was visibly shaking.

Following the initial sighting, several things have occurred. A second sighting behind the house (away from the road) where an upright creature was seen watching the youngest child. Noises and wood knocking come from the trees south of the house.

The noises begin barely perceptible and increase in volume if no one reacts. The family is visible to the woods through the family room windows while watching TV. One time the adult ignored the knocking sounds and they increased in volume until one of the children listening to music with headphones could hear them. If anyone reacts to the noises, they stop.

The family owns 44 acres which is mostly wooded. The property has a hidden pond in the woods which is teeming with frogs. I walked around the perimeter causing dozens of frogs to leap into the water.

Here is what really happened:

Do you want to know how to attract a bigfoot to your home?

1. Live in relative isolation.

2. Allow your children to play outside.

3. Turn on the television in a room that is visible to the woods.

4. Have a hidden pond on your property which is teeming with frogs – dozens of frogs, which leap into the water when you walk around the perimeter.

So who was out there:

1. scaring away wildlife, 2. surprising Miss B in the driveway, 3. peeping on a little child in the back yard and 4. banging so loud the knocking could be heard over muffled headphones and the broadcast of a big screen television?

That was a family group – Ward, June, Wally and Theodore. It's staggering to believe this troop has stayed together since the 1950's. Eisenhower Republicans, family values, that kind of stuff. The parents are really old. The sons never married.

Older son Wally is tanish brown with a hump on his back (it's a shoulder injury from track and field). His fur is short and clumped together. Miss B saw Wally in the hot morning sun when she was picking up the newspaper.

During the second sighting, younger son Theodore was seen watching the toddler in the back yard. Who doesn't love to watch little kids at play? And bigfoots are not perverts. We're Peeping Toms but we don't act on it. Never.

As for Ward and June, they maintain a nest in the woods high above the hidden pond. It's like owning a condo on Lake Amphibian.

Frogs are great protein and the pond is teeming with fat loud ones that just about jump into your mouth.

The noise?

That's Wally and Theodore messing around, beating the sticks, scaring up frogs with Eddie and Lumpy, until Ward has to shriek at them, "Boys! Wally! Beaver! Knock it off!"

*The BFRO.net website is the source for material used in this report. The report that appears here has been edited by Barry Bigfoot to conform with proper written English and the known facts.

SIGHTING TWELVE

Pre-dawn sighting by a newspaper delivery man near Pickaway (West Virginia)

MISSION STATEMENT: My name is Barry. I am a Sasquatch. In late June my cousin Dave and I scared a couple of campers near Seneca Rocks, West Virginia. In their haste to leave, one of the campers dropped his smart phone and I found it. As long as the camper allows his phone account to remain active, my blog to explain bigfoot sightings will continue.

Update: The camper read my first post and has agreed to continue funding his smart phone. Thank you Camper One!

BIGFOOT SIGHTINGS EXPLAINED

Here is a report* from a newspaper delivery man and his adult son:

My son and I were delivering newspapers in the Pickaway, WV area. We were on a one lane road. I pulled into a driveway to deliver a paper and as I was putting it in the box, my son [29 years old] says, look dad, a gorilla. I turned quickly to look. It was walking in the yard of the home towards the woods. We watched it for about 30 seconds as it left our view. I told my son there are no gorillas in WV., that's a bigfoot. It was about 7 feet tall with long arms, like a gorilla. It didn't seem to care about us at all. It just walked away. It was very hairy. We both got a real good look at it. We both got goose bumps. It was about 4 a.m. It was in September around the 5th. We looked every night in that area for the next 6 months but never saw it again.

Here is the report* filed by an investigator after speaking to the eyewitness:

I spoke with this witness at length. He said the animal's hair color was dark brown or black and was very long. Originally seen from approximately 15 feet. It moved away very casually, not ever turning to look at the witnesses in their truck.

Here is what really happened:

Sid wanted to get his hands on the latest newspaper. He had to check the sports section.

The night before he'd been watching the West Virginia game through an open window when the homeowner stood up, turned off the television and went to bed, with THREE MINUTES LEFT ON THE CLOCK!

Sid didn't find out the outcome of the game until I Googled it for him on my smart phone.

The Mountaineers won.

*The BFRO.net website is the source for material used in this report. The report that appears here has been edited by Barry Bigfoot to conform with proper written English and the known facts.

SIGHTING THIRTEEN

Nighttime encounter while training a coon hound outside Sinks Grove (West Virginia)

MISSION STATEMENT: My name is Barry. I am a Sasquatch. In late June my cousin Dave and I scared a couple of campers near Seneca Rocks, West Virginia. In their haste to leave, one of the campers dropped his smart phone and I found it. As long as the camper allows his phone account to remain active, my blog to explain bigfoot sightings will continue.Update: The camper read my first post and has agreed to continue funding his smart phone. Thank you Camper One!

BIGFOOT SIGHTINGS EXPLAINED

Here is a report* from two hunters:

A friend and I were out training my red-tick coon hound. We drove up a familiar dirt road. We drove to the end and were on our way back when the dog had struck out of the back of the truck. I got out, turned on my mining light and walked to the back of the truck. I opened the tailgate and let the dog loose. I stood beside the truck watching the dog sniff around in the road for a minute or so. I was shining my light around in the woods around me, when I saw a set of eyes looking at me. The eyes were a bluish green color and appeared to be 5-6 foot off the ground. I stood and watched it for at least 2-3 minutes wondering what it was. I hollered at my friend who was still sitting in the passenger side of the truck to come and look and tell me what he thought it was. We both stood there watching it, trying to figure out what it was. It's eyes would blink every now and then but it did not show any fear toward us or the dog. It was about 40 yards or so from us just enough so you could not see its body. We wanted to get a closer look so we decided to walk toward it. We only had one flashlight and for us to get closer we had to cross a small ditch and a broken down fence. I was trying to hold the light on the creature's eyes and hold the light so my friend did not fall. As we struggled to get across I noticed the eyes disappear. We hollered for the dog to come with us and we walked approx. 40-50 yards to where the creature was standing but did not see anything. We stood there for about 5 minutes talking and letting the dog sniff around but he acted a little nervous. We started walking back to the road. When we got back to the road we were about 60 yards behind the truck. As we were walking back to the truck, I was hollering for my dog to come on and I shined my light up in the woods from where we had left and the set of eyes returned. We looked at it for about 15 seconds, then noticed a second pair of eyes this time, The second pair of eyes were orange-red color and seemed to be taller than the first set. At this time we were spooked and made our way swiftly to the vehicle. When we got to the vehicle, we got inside and I shined my light out the window and both sets of eyes were staring at us blinking and showing no fear. I started up my truck and hollered for my dog to come on let's go. The dog jumped in the bed of the truck, I jumped out, ran to the back and hooked the dog up. I ran and got back in the truck. I shined the light out the window on the creatures, still staring at us, and my red-tick coon hound saw the creatures standing in the woods and started barking with every breath. The creatures continued to stare at us blinking and showing no fear. We decided it was time to get going. We started driving down off the hill. We drove a couple hundred yards and the dog was still barking with every breath. From the way the dog was acting, I felt they were following us. I shined my light up hill and sure enough, there they stood. I watched both of them follow us for about 1/2 mile.

Here is the report* filed by an investigator after speaking to the eyewitness:

Spoke to the witness on 16 August. His recollection of the event followed his written statement. I found his statement credible. He reported the source of the eye shine was never revealed by direct observation. He and his friend estimated the height from about 40 feet away, then proceeded to the spot the creature observed them from and confirmed the estimated height. The unknown creature was human-size but not human. The eye shine is not characteristic of humans in the visible spectrum, nor would being illuminated by a spotlight without protest. Night hunting is a normal activity for this part of the country. I can imagine no person who would have a spotlight directed at him without a verbal challenge of some sort. His first impulse would be to say,"Don't shoot!" Since the creatures were not observed directly we cannot say for certain what creatures were present. Only that they displayed curiosity and a lack of fear toward dog and man.

Here is what really happened:

Two men, accompanied by their coon dog, see eye shine. They attempt to move closer and the eye shine disappears. Later they see two sets of eyes, the second set higher above the ground than the first. The men get spooked and jump back into their truck. The dog, who has been running around with his nose on the ground, finally sees what the men have been seeing and goes nuts. The witnesses drive away and both sets of eyes follow the vehicle, first for a couple of hundred yards, then for a full half-mile, with the dog barking up a storm the whole way.

This all happened because Benny was standing a little too close to the road when the truck rolled by. The dog caught a whiff of Benny and alerted the driver and his friend. When the men got out of their truck, Benny became frightened and stood perfectly still. When they moved closer, he backed away.

Benny found Roscoe nearby and told him about the men. Roscoe, who is taller and wiser than Benny, walked his friend back to the site and whispered,

"Look at them. They're in the woods as much as we are. They know bears. They know deer. They think they know everything about the woods but they're having a really hard time figuring out what we are as long as we stay back here in the dark.

"Focus on the one with the light. He keeps blinking and rubbing his eyes. And the other guy, his knees just buckled. Did he just wet his pants?

"They're backing away. At least they're smart enough to be scared. Let's follow them for a while and really mess with their heads."

And that's exactly what happened in the woods outside Sinks Grove, West Virginia.

*The BFRO.net website is the source for material used in this report. The report that appears here has been edited by Barry Bigfoot to conform with proper written English and the known facts.

SIGHTING FOURTEEN

Husband and wife riding on an ATV spot a bigfoot near Becco (West Virginia)

MISSION STATEMENT: My name is Barry. I am a Sasquatch. In late June my cousin Dave and I scared a couple of campers near Seneca Rocks, West Virginia. In their haste to leave, one of the campers dropped his smart phone and I found it. As long as the camper allows his phone account to remain active, my blog to explain bigfoot sightings will continue.

Update: The camper read my first post and has agreed to continue funding his smart phone. Thank you Camper One!

BIGFOOT SIGHTINGS EXPLAINED

Here is a report* from a couple riding on an ATV who encounter a bigfoot:

My wife and I were riding an ATV in an abandoned strip mine. We came up over a small hill and approx. 25 – 30 yards in front of us and to the right of the trail stood a solid black creature ,approx.8 – 9 feet tall standing behind a tree that was only about 8 – 10 inches wide. I saw the creature first and my wife didn't notice it until I suddenly stopped the ATV and was trying to get it in reverse to turn around. She ask me what I was doing. I said, look, standing over there. When she saw the creature she started screaming "Oh my god no no no no!"I finally got the ATV turned around and left the area as fast as the ATV would run. My wife kept looking behind us to see if the creature was following us. Thank god it did not, but I still did not slow down until we were about two miles from the sighting area. I have totally lost intrest in outdoor activites that I once loved due to this experience.

I finally got up the nerve to go back to the sighting area. I had three other people with me, all heavily armed. We found some very strange things. Trees pushed over, large logs laying across the trail etc.

There have been other incidents n this area in the past couple of years. About five miles from *my sighting* a friend had a deer stolen by something that picked it up and walked off with it. Also, a local police officer said he saw a bigfoot run across the road in front of him about 2 – 3 miles from *my sighting* area.

Here is the report* filed by an investigator after speaking to the eyewitnesses:

I talked to the witnesses. He is a highway motorcycle patrolman and she is an official at a local museum.

In addition to what he reported, the following should be added:

The husband initially saw the creature about 100 yards away and thought that it was a fire burned stump that he was driving towards on his 4-wheeler. At about 50 yards, he realized that he was looking at a huge creature and he saw it turn it's head toward him. The husband was utterly terrified and shocked at the sheer size of the creature.

When describing the creature physically, the husband described the head shape as being similar to that of the 1967 Patterson-Gimlin film subject. The body was much wider across the shoulders than the waist. The creature had very shiny black hair that appeared to be groomed. There was sparse hair on the creature's face. Its forehead sloped back from its very dark eyes. The skin on its face was dark. He described it as "sinister and scary looking". He did not notice any associated odor. The female witness noted how very erect the posture of the creature was, and noticed how the creature was trying to hide behind a smaller tree.

The location is at the sight of an old strip mine site.

Here is what really happened:

First, I want to stress, the two most annoying humans are ATV riders and hunters. We see you. We hide from you. Is it that hard?

Sometimes we can't get out of the way fast enough from you fearless pricks on your monster four wheelers. And sometimes, in spite of that stupid orange hat on top of your camouflage greens and browns, we just don't see you. You don't have to shoot first and ask questions later. You have the gun, asswipe.

Manchild heard the ATV but he was out in the open in broad daylight. He tried to hide but where do you hide a nine foot monster who is walking across an abandoned strip mine, a vast territory completely cleared of timber, acreage so enormous you can pick it out on Google Map photos taken from outer space?

The husband was scared. The wife was scared. Manchild was scared. And sure, they got a great look at him, but they were safely aboard an expensive off-road escape vehicle and Manchild was trying to blend in behind a ten-inch-wide tree. Manchild has an 82-inch waistline.

The ATV wasn't stuck. The driver and his passenger weren't trapped. Manchild was kneeling down half a football field away. The ATV engine was running. The driver was grinding the gears. The witnesses had time to take written notes if they wanted to while Manchild cowered before them. They had the means to get two miles from the scene in a matter of moments and they kept acting like pussies.

And they still are. The husband gives up on the outdoors and returns to the site only when he is accompanied by three heavily armed men. Then he thumps his chest, speaking as an officer of the law and an expert witness and boasts about *his sighting,* where he describes Manchild as "Sinister."

I hope he falls off his bike.

*The BFRO.net website is the source for material used in this report. The report that appears here has been edited by Barry Bigfoot to conform with proper written English and the known facts.

SIGHTING FIFTEEN

The week in crime in Richwood, West Virginia from the Town Police Department crime report

MISSION STATEMENT: My name is Barry. I am a Sasquatch. In late June my cousin Dave and I scared a couple of campers near Seneca Rocks, West Virginia. In their haste to leave, one of the campers dropped his smart phone and I found it. As long as the camper allows his phone account to remain active, my blog to explain bigfoot sightings will continue.

Update: The camper read my first post and has agreed to continue funding his smart phone. Thank you Camper One!

BIGFOOT SIGHTINGS EXPLAINED

The following incidents are straight from the crime log of the police department in Richwood, West Virginia during the first week of July:

Petit Larceny — 600 Block Hillcrest Drive, SW July 02 between 6:15 a.m. and 7:51 a.m. A resident reported she placed her galvanized steel trash can by the curb for trash collection. She stated she went out later to collect the trash can and discovered it had been taken.

Responsible party: There is enough protein and fat in two cans of garbage to satisfy the nutritional needs of a growing Sasquatch for an entire day. Marvin didn't have to steal the can but he thinks of it as a ready-to-go kiddie meal.

Petit Larceny — 100 Block Patrick Street, SW July 04 4:46 a.m. A resident reported he observed a suspicious male in his back yard by his shed. The resident stated the man had run an extension cord from an electrical outlet in his shed and was attempting to charge his cell phone. The man fled the area.

Responsible party: That was me (Barry) and I was trying to charge my smart phone.

Open Door — TD Bank 308 Maple Avenue, West July 09 4:17 p.m. An alarm company reported a business alarm had been activated. Officer Todd Standing responded and located an unsecured door leading into the bank.

Officer Standing searched the inside of the bank and determined nothing appeared to be out of place.

The front door was secured prior to the officer leaving.

Responsible party: Officer Standing failed to notice that a huge bowl of candy sitting out on the receptionist's desk had been emptied. That was the handiwork of Big Tess, who has a real jones for sweets.

Suspicious Event — 100 Block Patrick Street, SE July 2 between 10:00 a.m. and 6:00 p.m. A resident reported she returned home and discovered her front door would not shut correctly. She stated someone may have attempted to gain entry but was unsuccessful. There were no other signs of an attempted forced entry into the residence.

Responsible party: If Marvin believes a home is dark and empty, he's a stickler for testing every door and window around the place. He broke the door trying to see if it was locked.

Grand Larceny — Community Center 120 Cherry Street, SE July 3 between 9:00 p.m. and 10:00 p.m. A citizen reported her bicycle was taken after she had left it unsecured in the area near the gazebo.

Responsible party: Cynthia always thought riding a bike looked easy until she tried it. She destroyed the vintage, 20-inch banana seat bicycle on her first attempt. Try submitting that claim to your insurance company.

Destruction of Property — Power Sub Station 405 Center Street, North Between July 2 at 5:00 p.m. and July 3 at 7:30 a.m. An employee found the chain link on two gates torn apart. The employee was unable to determine if anyone had entered the property or if anything was taken.

Responsible party: Marvin stopped at the Power Sub Station, too. He was a little too aggressive testing the chain.

Open Door — 100 Block Kingsley Road, SW July 2 1:19 p.m. Officer Standing observed a vehicle parked in front of a vacant house. While checking the exterior of the house the officer found the garage door open and a broken window above the back door lock.

The officer searched the interior of the home but found nothing to be disturbed.

Responsible party: Marvin says the back gate was open and the basement door wasn't secure, either.

Suspicious Event — 100 Block Tapawingo Road, SE July 2 8:45 p.m. A resident reported hearing suspicious noises in her basement.

Officers searched the exterior and interior of the residence, finding all doors and windows secure and nothing appeared to be disturbed.

Responsible party: Every door and window at that home was locked as tight as a drum and Marvin admits he may have huffed a little too loudly in frustration. Those grunts are what brought Officer Standing to the residence.

Grand Larceny — McDonalds 544 Maple Avenue, West July 4 11:51 p.m. A citizen reported his backpack, which contained his tablet notebook and an assortment of work tools, being stolen from his work vehicle. The backpack was left in the front seat of the unlocked vehicle for just a few minutes when the citizen realized it was missing. The backpack was subsequently found on Division Street but the tablet notebook was missing.

Responsible party: Chase is jealous because I have a smart phone. He's determined to get on-line but the citizen was quicker and canceled his service at 11:51 pm. at police headquarters.

Petit Larceny — 100 Block Patrick Street, SW Between July 2. A resident reported an "Echo" brand leaf blower had been taken from the shed in his back yard.

Responsible party: The item looked interesting to Marvin. I don't know what he's planning to do with a gas powered leaf blower. Did the resident report that his gasoline can was missing, too?

Burglary — 500 Block Kibler Circle, SW Between July

2-3 between 12:00 a.m. and 10:00 a.m. The owner of a home that is due to be razed returned to the home and discovered several items missing including a microwave, copper piping and the outdoor HVAC unit.

Responsible party: Two rednecks carted off the HVAC unit and the copper piping. Marvin saw them building a whiskey still out of some of the parts.

Still and all, Marvin made the top of the Most Wanted List in Richwood Township during the first week in July.

SIGHTING SIXTEEN

Two sightings outside rural home near Decola (West Virginia)

MISSION STATEMENT: My name is Barry. I am a Sasquatch. In late June my cousin Dave and I scared a couple of campers near Seneca Rocks, West Virginia. In their haste to leave, one of the campers dropped his smart phone and I found it. As long as the camper allows his phone account to remain active, my blog to explain bigfoot sightings will continue.

Update: The camper read my first post and has agreed to continue funding his smart phone. Thank you Camper One!

BIGFOOT SIGHTINGS EXPLAINED

Here is a report* from a husband and wife who had two encounters on their property:

My wife and I were watching television when the dogs started barking. Then within 5 minutes they got really quiet and went into their dog houses. We thought this was strange so we opened our back door toward where the dogs were barking and saw something near our mineral feeder for the cows. We live on a farm so we had an unused mineral feeder in the back yard.

It looked at first as if was on all 4 legs, and as big as the outline was, we assumed it was a bear, until it stood up on two legs. Now mind you we still thought it was a bear because you know bears do stand on there hind legs. We had our back porch light on so we could see it, but the thing we saw was still about maybe 80 ft away. Anyway what we thought was strange was after it stood up, it heard us at our back door and turned its head our way and when it did we saw big yellow like eyes. We looked at each other to make sure we both were seeing the same thing. Then we saw it's side arm move and the arm looked like it stretched below its knees. When it started to walk away, it walked mostly upright on 2 legs, swinging its arms still looking at us until it turned its head to the hayfield and walked away. To this day we still can't explain what we saw but we did see it.

The only thing we heard was really heavy breathing coming from this thing. And when we disturbed it, it looked at us and made like a gruff sound.

This is something we don't discuss with people. They may think we are nuts.

Here is the report* filed by an investigator after speaking to the eyewitness:

The witness stated the incident lasted approximately two minutes and happened around 10 PM. When the creature stood up, they immediately recognized it was not a bear. The height was about 7 feet, muscular build, covered with hair and approximately 50 yards from the house..

The creature and witnesses stared at each other for a considerable time. Finally, it grunted and walked toward the woods. She said it grunted twice more after entering the woods. The primary witness reported that she could smell a foul odor during the sighting. The creature walked with a purposeful stride swinging its arms and looking over its left shoulder until they lost sight of it.

The witnesses looked at each other and asked, "Did you see what I saw?" After confirming the sighting, they went inside as quickly as possible.

The witness and her spouse occasionally take walks through the fields behind their house. Sometimes she has a feeling of being watched and at the same time there is a lack of normal animal sounds.

INVESTIGATOR'S UPDATE:

I responded to the witness a second time. She had experienced another Class A sighting. This time the mother and her daughter were riding on an ATV through through their fields and noticed a deer stand was swaying from side to side.

Riding to an area where they could see better, the mother saw a large hair covered animal shaking the tree stand. It appeared to be between 8-9 feet tall, with dark colored hair.

The animal saw them and started running toward them. Her daughter, who was riding on back, was terrified by the situation and pounded her mother's back while yelling, "I want to go home, NOW!" They rode back home (about ½ mile) where the youngster jumped off the ATV before it stopped and ran inside the house.

The adult witness stated her husband returned to investigate but found nothing. The area where the deer stand is located is surrounded by open fields.

Here is what really happened:

Our community gets a real kick out of this report, especially the second incident.

Both sightings involved Danny.

The first sighting was another Peeping Tom situation gone awry. The dogs caught the scent of Danny, who was hiding behind the mineral feeder trying to watch television. The couple stepped on the back porch and saw Danny. He tried to pretend he was a tree stump but the ploy didn't work and he walked away in a huff.

The second sighting, that's a great one.

A hunter, whose unexpected appearance had forced Danny to hide up in a tree the year before, had returned to the farm and was crossing the property. Hunters are creatures of habit and seek out the same good locations year after year. Danny spotted the hunter first and decided to spook him. The frightened man dropped his rifle and Danny chased him into the tree stand.

He had him.

Danny grabbed the stand and shook the crap out of that hunter. The mother and daughter were eyewitnesses. Danny heard the ATV, turned on the mother and daughter and roared "Beat it!"

That was enough for the eyewitnesses and they shot away on their ATV. Danny released the tree stand and walked away.

The hunter finally got the courage to climb down from his perch, run across the field to his truck and change his drawers before the husband returned to investigate.

*The BFRO.net website is the source for material used in this report. The report that appears here has been edited by Barry Bigfoot to conform with proper written English and the known facts.

SIGHTING SEVENTEEN

Retired family doctor remembers daylight sighting as a teenager near Barboursville (West Virginia)

MISSION STATEMENT: My name is Barry. I am a Sasquatch. In late June my cousin Dave and I scared a couple of campers near Seneca Rocks, West Virginia. In their haste to leave, one of the campers dropped his smart phone and I found it. As long as the camper allows his phone account to remain active, my blog to explain bigfoot sightings will continue.

Update: The camper read my first post and has agreed to continue funding his smart phone. Thank you Camper One!

BIGFOOT SIGHTINGS EXPLAINED

Here is a report* from a retired physician:

I'm a 66 year-old physician living in Lillydale, New York. I grew up in Barboursville, W.Va. When I was 14 yo I was with my best friend (Rob Roberts, who grew up to be a veterinarian), also 14, and we were walking in the woods behind my grandparent's dairy farm. We had a 22G rifle with us and had been roaming around for about an hour when we came to a clearing at the top of a hill. We suddenly saw an animal neither of us recognized. When we first saw it, it was bent over doing something with its upper extremities. We were mesmerized for several minutes and did not move. It then seemed to become aware of us....what happened next really freaked us out. It stood up on back legs and looked right at us. We were terrified....it was very tall....blackish colored hair....also skinny in appearance with a tapered face. It was standing at the edge of a pine thicket. It turned away from us and jumped over a barbed wire fence. Even though we had a gun, we ran as fast as we could back to the farm house to relate the story to my grandfather. We saw an animal I've never seen, before or since. It was a tall and skinny and it was on two feet.

D. Howser, M.D.

Here is the report* filed by an investigator after speaking to the eyewitness:

In addition to what the witness has in the report, he added that it was a "frightening experience". Not because the animal was threatening in any way but because it was an animal neither boy could identify. Without any question it was tall, black and bipedal. To this day he will not enter the woods without being armed.

Its very common to hear that a sighting was a "life altering" experience and that the witness will think of the experience over his lifetime.

Here is what really happened:

Who could be a more probing and analytical witness than this guy? A trusted family physician for forty years, his sighting goes back to when he was fourteen years old and he and a friend were skulking around the woods for an hour with a 22 gauge rifle.

They walked through a clearing and came upon an animal out in the open. They could not figure out what they were looking at. It was not threatening. It was blackish in color and when the animal became aware of them, it stood high up on two legs and looked right at them. It was very tall and skinny and it had a tapered face.

It turned away and jumped over a barbed wire fence.

Who can jump over a barbed wire fence?

Steve McQueen could, but only on his motorcycle.

Stilts passed away not long ago but he spent most of his life around the grandfather's daily farm in Barboursville. On a bet, Stilts could jump over a fat milk cow from a standing start. There is no doubt that was him.

*The BFRO.net website is the source for material used in this report. The report that appears here has been edited by Barry Bigfoot to conform with proper written English and the known facts.

SIGHTING EIGHTEEN

Witness sees a bipedal creature on a country road outside Horner (West Virginia)

MISSION STATEMENT: My name is Barry. I am a Sasquatch. In late June my cousin Dave and I scared a couple of campers near Seneca Rocks, West Virginia. In their haste to leave, one of the campers dropped his smart phone and I found it. As long as the camper allows his phone account to remain active, my blog to explain bigfoot sightings will continue.

Update: The camper read my first post and has agreed to continue funding his smart phone. Thank you Camper One!

BIGFOOT SIGHTINGS EXPLAINED

Here is a report* made by the relative of a mother and daughter who had separate sightings:

The witness does not have internet access nor does she have typing skills. This report was submitted by her niece:

My aunt and my cousin both supposedly saw bigfoot along the highway. Both claimed that the creatures they have seen were certainly not human and not like any type of animal they have ever seen. They live in a very wooded country area with many wild animals. They have yet to see anything similar. They are very credible individuals.

The animal was standing by the road on two legs. It stared at her, very close to the vehicle with animal eyes that were oddly intelligent seeming.

My aunt and cousin had separate sightings. The daughter spotted the same creature in the same area.

It happened just after midnight.

Here is the report* filed by an investigator after speaking to the eyewitness:

I spoke to the witness. She reported the incident occurred in early fall. She was not sure of the actual date. She was driving alone at night going home. The animal was standing near a curve in the road at the end of a long straight.

Eyes reflecting like cat eyes made her slow down nearing the curve. The headlights illuminated not a deer but a bipedal creature covered in brown hair standing off the road. The road was a single lane, giving her a very good look from about 10 feet away.

It was over six feet tall, exactly how tall could not be estimated. She thought it was standing on the slope of the ditch, so it could have been between 6 and 7 feet tall. It watched her drive past. She was certain they made eye contact and reported it exposed its teeth, in either a smile or warning display. The teeth were all pointed, looking much like a mouth full of canine incisors.

She reported the face was not hair covered. It looked sort of human, with a wide nose, but not gorilla like. The skin color was dark-not black. she described seeing an Eskimo once on TV who had the same skin tone. The eyebrows were very bushy. The nostrils were flared.

The animal watched her drive by until out of sight. She thought it turned its head, not pivoting its upper body as in some other sighting reports. She got the impression it was intelligent. She did not feel threatened until after passing the creature. Once clear of the immediate area, a strong sense of fear overcame her.

In March a second sighting occurred within ½ mile of the first one. This time the daughter of this witness had a sighting of what seemed to be the same creature.

In conclusion, the witness gave a very good description of her sighting, with no hesitation. This level of detail and fluidity of conversation leads me to believe she was describing a living creature previously unknown to her.

Here is what really happened:

Big Tess has a habit of walking to Ruby's Restaurant after it closes for the evening and searching for food in the dumpster out back. The restaurant is a short distance from the Faith Tabernacle Church, where Deer Creek Lane meets Route 7.

Ruby's is a family restaurant that specializes in cake decorating and supplies. They make lot's of wedding cakes, birthday cakes and special occasion desserts, all to order.

Big Tess was returning from Ruby's on both occasions when she was spotted. Her stomach was bloated and her face was smeared with cake. That wasn't a warning display she made at the witness. Her teeth were covered with vanilla frosting.

*The BFRO.net website is the source for material used in this report. The report that appears here has been edited by Barry Bigfoot to conform with proper written English and the known facts.

SIGHTING NINETEEN

4:30 a.m. sighting by motorists on Ohio River Road outside Crown City (West Virginia)

MISSION STATEMENT: My name is Barry. I am a Sasquatch. In late June my cousin Dave and I scared a couple of campers near Seneca Rocks, West Virginia. In their haste to leave, one of the campers dropped his smart phone and I found it. As long as the camper allows his phone account to remain active, my blog to explain bigfoot sightings will continue.

Update: The camper read my first post and has agreed to continue funding his smart phone. Thank you Camper One!

BIGFOOT SIGHTINGS EXPLAINED

Here is a report* from a mother and son who had a sighting while driving to work:

ON OHIO RIVER ROAD, IT CAME ACROSS THERE AND WENT AWAY FROM THE PLANT

NEAREST TOWN: CROWN CITY

OBSERVED: MY SON AND I WERE ON OUR WAY TO WORK THURSDAY AUGUST 10. WE WERE ABOUT 2 MILES FROM OUR HOME IN W.VA. I TOLD HIM TO SLOW DOWN, THERE IS A MAN CROSSING THE ROAD AHEAD. WHEN WE GOT CLOSER TO IT I SAID WHAT IS THAT? MY SON WAS VERY FRIGHTENED AND SAID IT WAS BIGFOOT. WE WERE VERY SURPRISED IN SHOCK AND VERY SCARED. WE LEFT THE AREA AND WENT ON TO WORK. I CALLED MY HUSBAND AND TOLD HIM IMMEDIATELY WHAT WE HAD SEEN.

TIME AND CONDITIONS: 4:30 AM IT HAD RAINED THAT NIGHT AND WAS MUGGY AND SOMEWHAT FOGGY.

ONLY SOME LIGHTS FROM A OIL PLANT NEXT TO THE ROAD.

ENVIRONMENT: MAIN HIGHWAY, TRAIN TRACKS BESIDE THE ROAD, BESIDE A LARGE GAS PLANT. HOUSES AND A CHURCH ,RIVER JUST ACROSS THE TRACKS.

Here is the report* filed by an investigator after speaking to the eyewitness:

I met with this witness at the sighting location. The bigfoot crossed the road ahead of her from east to west, moving towards the railroad tracks.

Heavy brush thicket and thistles are between the road and the tracks. There is clear evidence of trails through the brush and no vertical obstructions. Witness reports figure appeared black and walked slumped over, with what appeared to be a limp.

Here is what really happened:

How about these two witnesses?

They go straight to work after seeing a bigfoot. They must have been more frightened of upper management than they were of a bigfoot.

On a wet and somewhat foggy night (4:30 a.m.), a mother and son are startled to see a big black man in the distance who is limping across the road.

When they get closer, the mother has time to ask out loud, "What is that?" and they become frightened. It slumps away while they continue safely down the highway in their Ford F-150 with the power locks on.

Go and wake *your* husband with that story.

Now ask yourself, why did the bigfoot cross the road?

Nester was headed for the river to scavenge for crayfish. He had to cross a highway, go over some railroad tracks and traverse a heavy brush thicket between the road and the tracks before he could get to the river.

Nester had made the decision to cross the road when he slipped on the wet pavement and wrenched his knee. That's why he crossed so slowly and "walked slumped over with what appeared to be a limp."

The witness woke her husband out of a sound sleep, at 4:30 in the morning, to share her story. I'm sure these additional details will help.

*The BFRO.net website is the source for material used in this report. The report that appears here has been edited by Barry Bigfoot to conform with proper written English and the known facts.

Rare Albino Raccoon Spotted in a West Virginia Trash Bin; Seeing One is Less Likely Than Getting Hit by Lightning

MISSION STATEMENT: My name is Barry. I am a Sasquatch. In late June my cousin Dave and I scared a couple of campers near Seneca Rocks, West Virginia. In their haste to leave, one of the campers dropped his smart phone and I found it. As long as the camper allows his phone account to remain active, my blog to explain bigfoot sightings will continue.

Update: The camper read my first post and has agreed to continue funding his smart phone. Thank you Camper One!

BIGFOOT SIGHTINGS EXPLAINED

Mountaineer State News Standard – August 12. by Dorothy Watters

For any modern-day Ahabs on the hunt for the elusive white raccoon, steer your ship to Pocock, West Virginia. One has been spotted trapped in a dumpster.

Grover Krantz discovered the furry white creature after hearing cries from a trash bin next to the Safeway.

Five young raccoons, including one albino, had climbed into the bin but couldn't get out. The rescue was a simple matter of putting a board in the dumpster so they could get away.

West Virginians can go their entire lives without glimpsing a white raccoon. The odds of spotting one have been estimated at 1 in 500,000 or even 1 in 750,000, making the encounter less likely than getting struck by lightning.

Here is what really happened:

Kindly old Mr. Krantz saved the elusive white raccoon. Lucky for Mr. Krantz, he didn't see Malvo hiding in the bushes. A few minutes earlier, Malvo had placed the raccoons in the bin for his own purposes. The odds of spotting Malvo — 1 in 3,000,000.

SIGHTING TWENTY-ONE

Close rural community is on alert in Nettie (West Virginia)

MISSION STATEMENT: My name is Barry. I am a Sasquatch. In late June my cousin Dave and I scared a couple of campers near Seneca Rocks, West Virginia. In their haste to leave, one of the campers dropped his smart phone and I found it. As long as the camper allows his phone account to remain active, my blog to explain bigfoot sightings will continue.

Update: The camper read my first post and has agreed to continue funding his smart phone. Thank you Camper One!

BIGFOOT SIGHTINGS EXPLAINED

Here is a report* from a community of witnesses:

Just two nights ago my brother who lives up the hollow from my house called a little after 8 p.m. to say he had seen something outside in his yard. It seemed to be turned in the direction of his chicken house, at an angle to him, where it could keep a lookout both toward his house and the driveway which passes on up further into the hollow where there is another house. I have another brother that lives right across the driveway from the first brother. This brother says that two nights before my brother saw what he did, he thought he saw something standing at the end of my 1st brother's screened in porch, my second brother was smoking on his screened in porch, and when he opened his screen door to get a better look, my 1st brother's pole light (which has a short in it) went out, and he couldn't see anything at all in that direction then. A few years ago, a third brother and neighbor to these other brothers, was walking in the dark without a light to my 2nd brother's house, and something screamed like a woman at him, and terrified him. This is a man standing 6' tall and over 300 lbs. My 1st brother is also 6' tall and over 300 lbs, and the creature he saw was taller and weighed more than he did. But he said it didn't seem to be fat. It had reddish brown fur-hair. He did not see the facial features due to the profile stance the creature was in and he said that it seemed to be aware that it, my brother yelled out loud, "What the heck is that!" and ran toward his front door that opens to his screened porch, he said that he felt the creature heard him and knew it had been observed and when he went to the front door and stepped out on the screened in porch, it was gone. The dogs didn't show up until my brother yelled for them. Last fall my daughter and myself were leaving her house, she lives at the bottom of my hill near the creek, when something that screamed like a women terrified us. Then I heard what sounded like someone hit the side of my house under the breezeway where my bedroom is located, and I have had what sounded to me like a man walking across my house again over where my bedroom is located and in a minute or two it retraced its steps. I was very frightened to say the least!

There are only a nine homes in this little valley that lies between two heavily wooded hills.

Here is the report* filed by an investigator after speaking to the eyewitness:

I spoke with this witness, her three brothers and their spouses at length. There seems to be definite, ongoing activity in this area with ample cover, food and water to support a small family group.

I advised them to keep in touch with me.

Here is what really happened:

There are so many brothers and sisters and cousins in this report who are married to brothers and sisters and cousins who are also witnesses that the whole effort is a waste of time.

*The BFRO.net website is the source for material used in this report. The report that appears here has been edited by Barry Bigfoot to conform with proper written English and the known facts.

SIGHTING TWENTY-TWO

Family group seen above visitors center on I-79 near Flatwoods (West Virginia)

MISSION STATEMENT: My name is Barry. I am a Sasquatch. In late June my cousin Dave and I scared a couple of campers near Seneca Rocks, West Virginia. In their haste to leave, one of the campers dropped his smart phone and I found it. As long as the camper allows his phone account to remain active, my blog to explain bigfoot sightings will continue.

Update: The camper read my first post and has agreed to continue funding his smart phone. Thank you Camper One!

BIGFOOT SIGHTINGS EXPLAINED

Here is a report* from a witness and his girlfriend who observed a family group:

My girlfriend and I were driving down from Morgantown, West Virginia at approximately 6:45 pm when she screamed, "Holy #%^*!, I just saw Bigfoot! Three of them, maybe four!" My girlfriend has great vision.

We backed up on the Interstate and raced to the spot.

The sighting took place at the Route 4 exit on Interstate 79. There is a visitor's center off to the left. We drove to where she saw them and parked. I spotted the group. They were way up at the top of the hill in the treeline. It consisted of 2 large and 2 smaller.

The larger appeared to be at least 7 to 8 foot tall. The smaller ones were 2 foot smaller. They were solid black in color. The group was approximately 150 ft away. The 2 larger were standing, the 2 smaller ones sitting. The group was moving back and forth. The 2 larger would squat then stand back up again, at least 4 times.

One of them moved downhill towards one of the smaller ones and bent over near it. There was enough light behind them for me to see arms and legs and what appeared to be a huge upper body on the largest one.

My girlfriend was very scared and said we needed to go. We got back in the car and watched the larger ones step into the trees. The smaller ones stood up and followed. We left at that point.

Here is the report* filed by an investigator after speaking to the eyewitness:

Witness said the sighting lasted about two minutes from the time they parked their car. The two larger animals seemed aware of being watched. The largest animal paid closest attention to the witness. The next paid more attention to the smaller pair and interacted with the small ones. The face was covered by hair. Body hair was long, 4-6 inches in length, could be seen hanging from the limbs when raised.The creature's arms came close to it's knees when standing upright.

The following weekend, the couple returned to the sighting location.
A small dog was brought to the sighting area. It "went wild" discovering what appeared to be a bedding area marked by vegetation crushed to the ground. It tugged at the leash wanting to proceed up the hill.

A week later, another trip to the sighting area.
A large rock was thrown at the couple. A large bipedal creature was seen at the top of the hill.

Here is what really happened:

A visitors center along a major highway is a welcome place to purchase a snack or take a break during a long drive, but to a family of bigfoot, it's a living classroom.

Lesson 1. Take the high ground. Humans adopted that strategy 35,000 years ago when they wiped out their closest cousins, the Neanderthals. That's a fact, Jack.

Lesson 2. Not only can a young bigfoot learn important do's and don't's by observing human activity from a vantage point, he can be right there when one or two sneak up the hill to smoke weed or make-out or relieve themselves away from the filthy restrooms. Great stuff. Very educational.

The witness and his girlfriend, the one with the great vision and the potty mouth, returned to the location two more times before a large rock was thrown at them. Take a hint, genius.

SIGHTING TWENTY-THREE

Washington Post: Ersatz Sasquatch Has Feet of Clay, Police Say (Virginia)

MISSION STATEMENT: My name is Barry. I am a Sasquatch. In late June my cousin Dave and I scared a couple of campers near Seneca Rocks, West Virginia. In their haste to leave, one of the campers dropped his smart phone and I found it. As long as the camper allows his phone account to remain active, my blog to explain bigfoot sightings will continue.

Update: The camper read my first post and has agreed to continue funding his smart phone. Thank you Camper One!

BIGFOOT SIGHTINGS EXPLAINED

Here is a report from *The Washington Post*:

By Leef Smith
Washington Post

An ape-like creature, covered in a tangle of leaves and branches, emerged yesterday from the bushes along a rural road in Fauquier County, prompting several very startled motorists to call police.

Bigfoot, they said, was afoot.

Virginia State Police didn't know what to make of the first sighting, at 3 a.m. Or the second. Or the third. So they sent out a trooper, and there he was, right there in the middle of Route 647. Sasquatch.

Sort of.

Officials say Bigfoot was being played by an 18-year-old prankster who, thinking himself clever, covered himself in fish netting and brush to resemble the infamous beastie more commonly thought to live in the Pacific Northwest.

"We get calls on bears in the road and different types of animals, but never has anybody called in and said they saw Bigfoot," said State Police Sgt. Perry Benshoof, who was not the lucky officer dispatched to the scene. "But that's what happened. One woman called up and said, `I don't know what I saw, but it looked like a small Bigfoot.'"

Police said the teenager's goal was not to frighten groggy motorists. The young man and an 18-year-old companion were on their way to play a practical joke on one of their sisters. She was house-sitting in nearby Marshall and apparently was headed for a shock.

The teenagers' prank was cut short when they tried to fool a passing police cruiser, officials said, and Bigfoot was unmasked.

Police said no laws were broken, so no charges were filed. The young men were sent home, and the officer didn't take down their names.

"Other than being in the roadway and walking in front of cars, they violated no laws," Benshoof said with a sigh.

Here is what really happened:

One woman called up and said, `I don't know what I saw, but it looked like a small Bigfoot.'

The Virginia State Police send out a patrol car and the officer detains two fools as they emerge from the bushes along rural Route 647.

The Washington Post picks up this *ha ha* story from nearby Fauquier County, Virginia. This is some serious, investigative journalism.

Can you imagine Leef Smith of *The Washington Post* asking his editor to take this subject seriously? Print journalism jobs are tough enough to get without broaching this topic.

And what would the *The Washington Post* do if it turned its' impressive "Watergate" energies on this mystery?

Have you ever heard of a college or university, government agency, police department or branch of the armed services earmarking grant money, funds or budget dollars towards this? Would you risk your tenure, status, rank or government job putting your name behind this one?

What institution has sponsored and equipped any scientific expedition or committed any effort or resources to document, or refute, the existence of a North American primate?

Instead, skeptics use ignorance of the primary data and the resultant hoaxes to pronounce baseless and cynical condemnation of the subject. They say evidence has been weighed and measured and found wanting.

Weighed and measured. By whom? When? Where?

It's a mystery.

A beacon of light is the work of professor Jeff Meldrum, Ph.D. (*Sasquatch: Legend Meets Science*).

Thanks Jeff.

I'll give credit where credit is due.

Both the Virginia State Police and *The Washington Post* investigated this sighting and got it right.

SIGHTING TWENTY-FOUR

ATV rider has a daylight encounter on his family farm near Wintergreen Resort (Virginia)

MISSION STATEMENT: My name is Barry. I am a Sasquatch. In late June my cousin Dave and I scared a couple of campers near Seneca Rocks, West Virginia. In their haste to leave, one of the campers dropped his smart phone and I found it. As long as the camper allows his phone account to remain active, my blog to explain bigfoot sightings will continue.

Update: The camper read my first post and has agreed to continue funding his smart phone. Thank you Camper One!

BIGFOOT SIGHTINGS EXPLAINED

Here is a report* from an experienced hunter:

I was ridding my atv on the family farm going down an old washed out road which you can't drive fast on. As I started down the road looking down at the road then looking up down the road something caught my eye about 150 to 200 yards down this road. The sun was to my left shining across this road to the right as I looked down this narrow road there was a reflection of the light coming off the fur of something that I never had seen before,it was tall and massive. For that split second I saw it. The way the suns reflection came off of this thing it look almost silver. But being a hunter (I hunt this land all the time) There isn't anything silver in color. And that the sun coming off the back of a black turkey can look silver. So that's what caught my eye. This animal went back in to the woods back to the right. I worked my way down to where I thought I saw it. I turned my atv off and smoked a cig. Listing for any thing and about 5 min. had past and I heard something big running away from my direction breaking big tree limbs. (It was way louder than a deer running through the thickets). I could hear this for about 1 to 2 seconds and then it went quiet again. If I had to guess how far away it was I would say about 50 to 60 yards away from me when I first heard the running. (You cant see more than 20 yards in to this thickets from where I was at. (Hunting season end for general firearms 10 days before this so the deer are still alert.) Then it seemed like a couple of min. later I heard two big bangs like someone hitting a stick against a tree or log then the hair on the back of my neck stood up.Then there was the snorting of the deer that came from the thicket right after that. (When a deer snorts from my experience in the woods during the day they see you and snort once or twice and then they take off leaving you just to see there white tail waving at you as they go out of sight.) But there must have been 4 or 5 white tail in there all of them snorting and stomping the ground and they were real loud.The deer did this for about what seamed to be more than a min.then I heard them take off running. And that's when I decided it was time for me to leave too.I went home and told my wife about what had just happened and she couldn't believe it and was surprised at what I told her and ask if it was bear? I told her I never saw a beer in the woods and it seamed way to big to be a black bear.So the next day I took a camera in where I heard this animal and took pictures of what I believe to be footprints and some hair that was left on a tree limb about 5 1/2 feet off the ground

Here is the report* filed by an investigator after speaking to the eyewitness:

Witness is an experienced hunter. He estimates the creature to be near eight feet tall and to weigh over 500 lbs. The witnesses' estimate of size eliminates a bear. He has seen plenty of bears at that distance and knows what he saw was far larger. The sighting was brief but made a distinct and lasting impression on the witness.

Here is what really happened:

It was tall and massive. He saw it for a split second. A reflection came off the fur and it looked almost silver.

That's what caught his eye. The animal went into the woods to the right and the rider worked his way down to where he thought he saw it. He turned off his ATV and smoked a "cig". He heard two big bangs like someone hitting a stick against a tree or log, then the hair on the back his neck stood up. He heard something big running away and breaking big tree limbs but he could not see more than 20 yards into the thicket.

He said there must have been four or five white tail deer in there, all of them snorting and stomping the ground and they were really loud. The deer did this for more than a minute, then took off running.

All this occurred when the witness "was ridding my ATV on the family farm." For a split second, he sees "something that I never had seen before, it was tall and massive." He turns off the ATV and "smokes a cig".

How cool is this witness, all alone on his ATV, out in the wild with something tall and massive only 50 yards away and he's calmly pulling on his Marlboro light?

He had seen plenty of bears. He knew it was far larger.

The witness was correct. Almost eight feet tall and weighing 505 pounds, Sugar Ray was nervously cowering in the thick brush, desperate to remain hidden.

Sugar Ray and Leonard had been tracking deer when the ATV rider crashed their hunt. They took cover with six deer sandwiched between them and the Marlboro man.

Hiding didn't seem to work. The Marlboro man continued to stand by his ATV and pull on his "cig,"

Five minutes elapsed.

Making a break for it seemed to be the answer. Leonard took a branch and smacked a tree behind the Marlboro man, his signal to Ray that it was time to go. Ray went one way and Leonard went the other.

The knock shocked the smoker out of his reverie and "the hair on the back of his neck stood up". The stupid deer, already extremely upset by the presence of Sugar Ray and Leonard, took advantage of their exit and ran the other way.

The Marlboro man went home and told his wife everything that had happened.

She couldn't believe it. The story sounded too extraordinary to be true. Eight feet tall? 500 pounds? What was he smoking out there?

The Marlboro man returned to the site the next day to take photos. What good are photos, or footprints, or hair samples for that matter?

He might as well get an affidavit from one of the deer.

*The BFRO.net.website is the source for material used in this report. The report that appears here has been edited by Barry Bigfoot to conform with proper written English and the known facts.

SIGHTING TWENTY-FIVE

Runner shadowed by biped through heavy forest near Westlake Corner (Virginia)

MISSION STATEMENT: My name is Barry. I am a Sasquatch. In late June my cousin Dave and I scared a couple of campers near Seneca Rocks, West Virginia. In their haste to leave, one of the campers dropped his smart phone and I found it. As long as the camper allows his phone account to remain active, my blog to explain bigfoot sightings will continue.

Update: The camper read my first post and has agreed to continue funding his smart phone. Thank you Camper One!

BIGFOOT SIGHTINGS EXPLAINED

Here is a report* from a long distance runner:

I am an avid runner. I run close to 50 miles a week every week. I often run the exact same route. When I trail run I have been followed by deer and other wildlife that comes up from time to time. However, today was different. First I was not on a trail but on a country road near my house. I crossed a main road and was headed out to my turn around point. There is a thick wooded area on the right hand of the road. I heard something in the woods and thought maybe it was a deer or a dog. I kept running but the noise kept happening. It was like someone was in the woods just out of sight running in the leaves as I was running on the road. I would slow down and it would slow down. I would speed up and it would speed up. When I passed a house the noise would stop for a few yards and then pick back up again in the wooded areas. I am an avid hunter. This really sounded like a person or something like a person running along in the woods as I ran the road. Thing is the wooded side of the road is very up and down with several deep drop offs. So whatever was keeping pace with me was able to navigate them with no problem at all. I run a 9 minute mile pace. So whatever was following me in the woods had to keep that pace yet in the woods and the deep valley areas. Maybe I was hearing things but it would slow down and speed up when I did. It would go around the house areas and then come back to shadow me in the woods.

This was around 9:30 AM and was extreme overcast weather from a lingering storm over the last few days of rain. Rolling hills around the mountains.

Here is the report* filed by an investigator after speaking to the eyewitness:

Witness logs 40 miles and more a week, runs trails and roads on the same routes on a routine basis, has seen plenty of bears and heard them in the woods and is occasionally followed for short distances by deer when he runs. Encounter was not on a trail or in the woods, but along a country road. Visibility into the woods along the road was poor. The road is mostly wooded to his turn around point. He began to hear something in the woods, slowed to look and see if it was a deer or dog but could see nothing. He noticed at this time that the noise following him also slowed down. As he sped up again, so did the sound of something pacing him. It sounded like a person running in the leaves, but much louder and he could hear branches and other debris breaking easily as the subject followed. He decided it was someone playing around with him and just kept running. When he made it to the first house the noise stopped and Mr. W. continued his run. After passing the house, and about 20 yards farther along the road, the noise picked up again, just as he had heard it before. He believes whatever was tailing him had gone around the house, possibly to stay out of sight. As he continued his run, he would occasionally slow down, or even come to a full stop, and the shadowing sounds would slow or stop with him. These shadowing sounds continued steadily and then stopped. If it was a person he would have to navigate creeks, valleys, and thick forest as if he were running down the side of a road. The witness runs at a 9 minute per mile pace and whatever was in the woods kept pace with him over rough terrain. He estimates his shadower was about 50 yards away in the woods because he could not see anything with the fog.

He has run this route repeatedly since that day but has not heard it again.

Here is what really happened:

If you have to train, you want to train with someone who's going to push you a little.

Sometimes you wait in the bushes for a runner to pass and you tail him, for nine miles or so. Your target is listening to music through ear buds or he's under the spell of his "runner's high" so he won't notice. Or will he?

This runner was not imagining things.

Only a deaf person would have missed all the noise Bruce was making.

It was easy to miss the sight of him, however, because it was foggy outside and Bruce is an albino bigfoot. Very rare. Only 9 in North America and Canada. (See Pennsylvania White Bigfoot Sighting on YouTube. Pennsylvania White is Bruce's full brother.)

Bruce is a prodigy at track and field. Think Jesse Owens, Usain Bolt, Bruce Jenner (pre-Caitlyn).

But hey, every Sasquatch is a superior athlete to a certain degree, until we grow to our full size (7-9 feet).

High hurdles, sprints, long distances, uphill, downhill, over rocks, through bushes, up a tree. No problemo.

Bruce stopped tailing women at the beginning of his training program.

The very first lady he followed, a feisty little gal with extremely poor eyesight, sprayed him with mace, kicked him in the shins and started blowing a whistle.

See: Pennsylvania White Bigfoot Sighting on YouTube

*The BFRO.net website is the source for material used in this report. The report that appears here has been edited by Barry Bigfoot to conform with proper written English and the known facts.

SIGHTING TWENTY-SIX

Manlike figure seen in the trees by soldiers on guard duty at Radford Army Ammunition Plant (Virginia)

MISSION STATEMENT: My name is Barry. I am a Sasquatch. In late June my cousin Dave and I scared a couple of campers near Seneca Rocks, West Virginia. In their haste to leave, one of the campers dropped his smart phone and I found it. As long as the camper allows his phone account to remain active, my blog to explain bigfoot sightings will continue.

Update: The camper read my first post and has agreed to continue funding his smart phone. Thank you Camper One!

BIGFOOT SIGHTINGS EXPLAINED

Here is a report* from a soldier serving 2-4 a.m. guard duty:

This happened during a training operation. No one outside of the military had access to this location. I had a very compelling sighting of what can only be described as a Bigfoot. I am willing to tell my story once I am contacted and also I know two soldiers that saw the same being. I can assure you that I am 100 percent honest with what I saw and that I can provide proof of my credentials and location.

All of the witnesses including myself said that the being had been in the trees over top of us and it was dead quiet just before and during the sighting. We were on watch at the same time during a training operation.

It was very dark that particular night. It was cold. The area is heavy wooded, with plenty of water sources, food sources, wildlife and changes in elevation.

Here is the report* filed by an investigator after speaking to the eyewitness:

After a lengthy phone conversation with the witness, the following information may be added to his report:

During a training event, after disembarking and maneuvering through the training ranges, his unit set up a bivouac to sleep for the night.

While pulling guard duty with two other soldiers between 2 and 4 a.m. the witness looked up from his seated position and saw a large human shape standing in the trees above him.

He estimates the figure was 30 feet from him and above him on a 45 degree angle. It's body was heavily built and the height was between 7 and 8 feet. It was silhouetted against the starlit sky and stood out clearly.

It appeared to be holding onto the trees with long outstretched arms but he could not make out what its feet were resting on.

The soldier blinked his eyes to test and clear his vision and the figure remained. He blinked his eyes a second time and saw the figure move silently from one large tree to the next.

He blinked his eyes a third time and the figure vanished from sight.

In the morning, the soldier made no mention of his observation during the unit's meeting before the unit moved out. Later, a soldier who'd been on watch at a location away from the witness asked if anyone had seen something in the trees the night before.

A third soldier responded in the affirmative and described a large manlike figure moving silently through the trees above the unit's position. He was observing from a location apart from the first two men.

They came to the conclusion they had seen the same figure, high above their posts, traversing silently through the old growth trees and circling their unit's position.

The first witness has been honorably discharged, the second is deployed to Afghanistan and unavailable for comment and the third has fallen out of contact.

Here is what really happened:

Their perimeter was clearly being violated and all three soldiers, who were on guard duty and sworn to protect their country, saw "a large human shape" from different positions as it moved gracefully above them. Not one of them offered a challenge. No report was sent up the chain of command.

Is it any wonder these guys don't want to put their names on UFO reports either?

*The BFRO.net website is the source for material used in this report. The report that appears here has been edited by Barry Bigfoot to conform with proper written English and the known facts.

SIGHTING TWENTY-SEVEN

Driver sees large animal from the waist up along the roadside in Ararat (Virginia)

MISSION STATEMENT: My name is Barry. I am a Sasquatch. In late June my cousin Dave and I scared a couple of campers near Seneca Rocks, West Virginia. In their haste to leave, one of the campers dropped his smart phone and I found it. As long as the camper allows his phone account to remain active, my blog to explain bigfoot sightings will continue.

Update: The camper read my first post and has agreed to continue funding his smart phone. Thank you Camper One!

BIGFOOT SIGHTINGS EXPLAINED

Here is a report* from a driver who passed a motionless figure:

I had passed that point about an hour earlier and the area was loaded with deer. Had to slow way down to avoid a collision. There were at least 8 there at 9 pm.

On the way back Eastbound down the mountain I slowed way down as I approached the area. I looked carefully to avoid any animal contact

In the brights, as I looked right I saw a yellow reflection first. As I got closer, I saw the top part of an obviously large creature.

Its arms were spread out to either side. I could see hair hanging from the arms. The elbows were bent slightly. The head appeared flat-faced, huge and slightly higher at the rear. The shoulders were broad. The color was dark. A slight sulfurous odor was detected.

The steep bank hid most of the creature. It was perfectly still. I almost felt it thought it was not visible to passing vehicles.

I went back to the area about 10 days later and saw some scuff marks on the bank side. This area is criss-crossed by many deep ravines and creeks, heavy woods.

Here is the report* filed by an investigator after speaking to the eyewitness:

After further investigation, witness added the following:

The closest I got was probably about 15', as the car was even with the thing. I've seen black bears in the wild. There isn't any way a bear could be shaped remotely like the thing I saw.The arms were LONG and not thick.The hair was about 6".The eye shine was from a ways up the road. As I pulled even the face was pointed straight across the road.The angle of the bent elbows was about 20 degrees.To tell you the truth, I was kind of stunned, numb, and not quite able to digest it.I'm sure I would have seen nothing had I not slowed down to 25 or so mph and been looking for deer.

I think the thing was pretending to be a bush.

Here is what really happened:

Donna is well versed in our basic survival techniques. For example, if you are spotted and you can't run:

(1) Act like a tree.

Donna is red and brown. She can stand perfectly still if she has to, but she's way too tall to be mistaken for a bush.

She might be mistaken for a dogwood, with her arms extended away from her sides, but a more prudent tactic:

(2) Remember to DUCK!

*The BFRO.net website is the source for material used in this report. The · report that appears here has been edited by Barry Bigfoot to conform with proper written English and the known facts.

SIGHTING TWENTY-EIGHT

Sasquatch turns on homeowner after he orders his son to fire shotgun near
Massanutten (Virginia)

MISSION STATEMENT: My name is Barry. I am a Sasquatch. In late June my cousin Dave and I scared a couple of campers near Seneca Rocks, West Virginia. In their haste to leave, one of the campers dropped his smart phone and I found it. As long as the camper allows his phone account to remain active, my blog to explain bigfoot sightings will continue.

Update: The camper read my first post and has agreed to continue funding his smart phone. Thank you Camper One!

BIGFOOT SIGHTINGS EXPLAINED

Here is a report* from a witness who ordered his son to shoot a bigfoot.

It was about 3 a.m. I heard a noise as if something fell that was heavy, a thud sound in the back of my house. I thought it might be a bear or burglar. Me and my 29 year old son went out to investigate. my son had a shotgun. I saw a deer run as if it was being chased. Then I saw a huge figure coming out of the woods. This thing was at least 8 feet tall. I could not believe this. I screamed out to this thing to stop. It came towards us running. I told my son to shoot. He shot in its direction. It then ran to my left flank and continued to come toward us. We ran back towards the house. I was in terror because the thing was shaped like a man but was covered with hair. I do not believe in Bigfoot but I cannot explain this. I stopped and watched it walk away into the light and it was huge and there was an odor that really stunk in the air. It stayed in sight for about 5 minutes before it went into the woods. I investigated the next day and there are footprints that are about 18 to 20 inches in the field. Unless this is a hoax and someone was in a costume? We fired on this thing and it made a huffing noise and a shriek sound. I have followed some the prints and there is long hair brown and gray back in the woods. I have had more noise and sightings in the woods behind my home. I live in the country and unless someone is doing this in a costume then this is the real bigfoot. There is also an underground tunnel dug into the side of a creek bed. The prints lead into the tunnel and I am not going in there. It is not a bear because a bear would never charge a gun shot.

Here is the report* filed by an investigator after speaking to the eyewitness:

Witness believed a prowler was visiting his farm at night and causing trouble. He managed to track large bipedal steps through dew and tall grass on a number of occasions. And frequently those tracks would take a circuitous route away from this house before entering the forest.

On the night of his encounter, he and his eldest son went into the backyard to confront a suspected prowler. Once there, a deer ran toward the witness, from the forested edge of a soy bean field, about 50 yards wide. He was surprised that a deer actually ran toward him and his son, who was standing 40 feet to his right.

Witness grew panicked and ordered his son to fire his shotgun.

The son confirms that he fired his shotgun, but high and in the direction of the wood line. He said it was too dark to see well but he did clearly hear the sound of running feet approaching. He described the sound as loud and as heavy as if a horse were running toward them.

After the gun shot, the creature stopped just 15 feet short of where the witness stood. In the seconds before he turned and ran back into his house, he saw a massive creature, four feet wide, that dropped from two legs to a three-point crouch, placing one hand on the ground. And while it was too dark to make out details of the face, he could see well enough to discern a surprised look on the animal's face as it looked at him, panting heavily.

Witness did not fire his weapon but instead turned and ran as fast as he could back around his house and in through the front door. His son was immediately behind him. The wife of the witness later conveyed that her husband's face was blanched white with a look of terror and for some time he was unable to verbalize clearly. When he had calmed enough to tell her what he'd seen, he could only describe it as a big hairy demon.

Common occurrences include loud slaps on the side of his home during the night. Large objects, like riding lawn mowers or trailers in his yard, mysteriously relocating overnight. Loud choruses of wailing howls that break out in remote forests around his farm, occasionally waking his family from sleep. A young daughter reported seeing a large, hairy man outside the window. Witness found the upper window onto his back porch smashed in and a bag of garbage stored there had gone missing. Some time after this, the door onto the back porch was ripped apart and more trash bags were stolen from the porch.

On another occasion he and his son were in their front yard when rocks were thrown at them from the woods behind their house. Several rocks landed before his son began to pick the rocks up and throw them back. but his son's rocks fell well short of the tree line, which was over 100 yards away. More rocks came from the forest, only much more rapidly than before. and his son were forced to retreat into their home. Since then, they have occasionally heard rocks hitting the roof of their home during the night.

Witness once observed what he thought was a very large Marine wearing a backpack and ghillie suit and walking along the road in front of his house. The Marine simply disappeared into the darkness.

A neighbor, a long time resident of the area, admitted to multiple instances of seeing the creature over the course of 25 years. When I contacted the neighbor he was not interested in going on the record with his story and did not want to encourage anyone who might come and disturb the creature.

The witness believes in hindsight it was a mistake to fire a weapon around the creature. He feels it probably meant no harm and that it was attempting to flee the encounter but was frightened and confused by the gun fire incident.

Here is what really happened:

Dazed and confused.

That about sums it up this sighting. The witness was frightened and confused. So was the bigfoot. And so was the deer.

Just another case of shooting first and asking questions later.

Dodger had overstayed his welcome. The home had become an easy source for quality television, garbage raids and harmless pranks until the son opened fire.

It was really dark. The son had been wise to fire off a warning shot. It was the son and not his stressed out old man who would have to go to prison if he killed a petty thief.

Dodger was trailing a deer as it walked into the homeowner's yard. The deer had decided it was safer to move towards the men than it was to wait for Dodger.

At the sound of the rifle, Dodger stepped forward instead of dropping into a defensive position or turning away. Who knows how one will react to the sound of gun fire? After all this time, the homeowner had never resorted to violence. Dodger is absolutely thrilled the father wasn't holding the gun.

Dodger got up and walked away. For five minutes he looked back longingly before heading into the forest. Now for certain he was going to miss the final episode of "Breaking Bad".

SIGHTING TWENTY-NINE

Finding Bigfoot on Animal Planet (Earth)

MISSION STATEMENT: My name is Barry. I am a Sasquatch. In late June my cousin Dave and I scared a couple of campers near Seneca Rocks, West Virginia. In their haste to leave, one of the campers dropped his smart phone and I found it. As long as the camper allows his phone account to remain active, my blog to explain bigfoot sightings will continue.

Update: The camper read my first post and has agreed to continue funding his smart phone. Thank you Camper One!

BIGFOOT SIGHTINGS EXPLAINED

What are you guys doing? We see you coming from two miles away. You come in the morning and you come back at night, banging your lights and your audio equipment.

And why are you guys whispering?

One of you takes a whack at a tree with a branch or a baseball bat. A rotten branch falls from a decaying tree not far from where we are hiding and suddenly it's a chorus of "Woo woo, that must be them Bobo!"

Kudos for your service. You are doing a remarkable job moving this topic a notch closer to sanity on the crazy meter.

Thank you for the treats and thank you for the entertainment.

SIGHTING THIRTY

Campers see their trash bags taken by a figure on two legs outside Dooms (Virginia)

MISSION STATEMENT: My name is Barry. I am a Sasquatch. In late June my cousin Dave and I scared a couple of campers near Seneca Rocks, West Virginia. In their haste to leave, one of the campers dropped his smart phone and I found it. As long as the camper allows his phone account to remain active, my blog to explain bigfoot sightings will continue.

Update: The camper read my first post and has agreed to continue funding his smart phone. Thank you Camper One!

BIGFOOT SIGHTINGS EXPLAINED

Here is a report* from a camper who watched a figure on two legs take his trash bags down from a secure location.

We were sleeping in the bed of our truck when my wife woke up and saw something big walk past the truck. It went over to where I had our trash bags (10-20 feet from the truck) tied up in a tree to keep animals away.The bags contained the remains of a chicken we had cooked over the fire, plus other garbage.I am 5'8" and had the bags tied up high enough that I could not reach them. You could see the white bags moving as something reached up and grabbed one of the bags out of the tree. I had my wife crawl through the window into the cab and honk the horn. It just turned and looked at us but did not run off. It always stayed on two legs and looked wider and taller than a bear. After taking one bag it went off into the woods and you could hear it tearing open the bag and eating the contents. About a half hour later it came back into the camp and took the other bag out of the tree.I had a flash light but did not leave the truck to get a good look at it. We could only see its shape when it was getting the bags. After taking the last bag and leaving, I had my wife hold the pistol while I got out and threw everything into the truck and we left and spent the rest of the night in a rest stop off interstate 81.

We did not notice any smell. It made no noise and we saw no footprints but area was hard ground and dry where we camped. It was between 12-2 AM, partly cloudy, partial moon. Relatively flat, forested with small creeks, a wilderness area

Here is the report* filed by an investigator after speaking to the eyewitness:

The witness and his wife repeated the encounter in detail.

The garbage bags were white and estimated to be hung 9 to 10 feet from the ground. The animal entered the camp sometime after midnight. The witness remembers it was late.

During the entire time of the encounter the animal moved bipedal on two legs and never went down to all fours. It was seen swatting at the garbage bags until it grabbed hold of one of the bags. It then walked off into the woods with the garbage bag at an estimated 5 to 6 feet from the ground while the animal was carrying it.

The animal looked bigger then a bear. There was no smell associated with the animal and no tracks found.

The witness did not follow the animal into the woods after it took the garbage bags. No features could be made out and the vehicle had the rear facing toward the hanging garbage bags, so the headlamps could not be illuminated on the animal.

Here is what really happened:

American fast food, pure and simple. Super size the meal and ask for it to go, straight into the woods. Hanging bags of food above the ground is like waving a Golden Arches sign at our pal Sammy.

Sammy loved the chicken but said the vegetables could have used a little salt.

*The BFRO.net website is the source for material used in this report. The report that appears here has been edited by Barry Bigfoot to conform with proper written English and the known facts.

SIGHTING THIRTY-ONE

8-ft. creature effortlessly negotiates 4-ft. barbed wire fence north of Sugar Grove (Virginia)

MISSION STATEMENT: My name is Barry. I am a Sasquatch. In late June my cousin Dave and I scared a couple of campers near Seneca Rocks, West Virginia. In their haste to leave, one of the campers dropped his smart phone and I found it. As long as the camper allows his phone account to remain active, my blog to explain bigfoot sightings will continue.

Update: The camper read my first post and has agreed to continue funding his smart phone. Thank you Camper One!

BIGFOOT SIGHTINGS EXPLAINED

Here is a report* from a driver who saw a bigfoot step over a four foot fence.

I had the most incredible thing happen to me on the morning of November 4.

It was a very warm and foggy morning. What I saw next completely caught me off guard.

As I exited the last curve, I could not believe what I was seeing. Standing on the side of the road I was 20 yards from what I know was bigfoot.

It, he, was crossing a three strand barbed wired fence in one stride. This thing had to be 7 and a half to 8 feet tall. It walked with kind of a lumber. It never once looked at me, as I had stopped in the middle of the road to watch it walk away.

The hair was a reddish brown and about 4 inches long. It had no neck. The arms were very long, about three inches below its knees, but in proportion with its body. I have hunted these mountains for years and had heard of legends of a hairy beast man. I had never seen anything like I was seeing.

6:30 am, daybreak but still dark in places. patchy fog and rain. mountain, open field, and pine tree patches. new river just about a mile down the hill with lots of caves

OTHER STORIES: I heard in the early 90's, a friend of mine saw what he described as a bigfoot about 5 miles north on the same highway. My grandfather, who was a very well known outdoorsman and an honest man, told me that back in the late 80s he was feeding the animals one summer evening around 7:30 pm. He watched what he said was 2 hairy beasts in the open field adjacent to his property for 10 minutes. His property is only a few miles as the crow flies from my sighting.

Here is the report* filed by an investigator after speaking to the eyewitness:

Witness is a 35 year-old man. The animal crossed a fence approximately 4-ft tall. The animal was around 8-ft tall.

When it stepped over the fence, it put one hand on top of a fence post to steady itself and stepped over.

The distance to the animal upon first sight was around 75 yards. At the closest point, the witness and animal were within 20 yards.

He stated at no time did the animal seem worried or rush to get away from him. It walked smoothly away into the morning fog. He considered using his cell phone camera to photograph it but by the time he was ready the creature looked like a stump in the open distance with nothing to provide a measure of size around it.

Here is what really happened:

The witness saw Sanford "put one hand on the fence post to steady himself" before stepping over 4 feet of barbed wire. What the witness failed to notice was that Sanford was juggling three eggs and a chicken at the same time.

*The BFRO.net website is the source for material used in this report. The report that appears here has been edited by Barry Bigfoot to conform with proper written English and the known facts.

SIGHTING THIRTY-TWO

Paul Freeman bigfoot video (Washington State)

MISSION STATEMENT: My name is Barry. I am a Sasquatch. In late June my cousin Dave and I scared a couple of campers near Seneca Rocks, West Virginia. In their haste to leave, one of the campers dropped his smart phone and I found it. As long as the camper allows his phone account to remain active, my blog to explain bigfoot sightings will continue.

Update: The camper read my first post and has agreed to continue funding his smart phone. Thank you Camper One!

BIGFOOT SIGHTINGS EXPLAINED

God bless Paul Freeman.

He died a mocked man but all he did was document the protective instincts of a mother with her child, albeit a very large mother with a pot belly who was covered with hair from head to toe.

Paul was a pioneer researcher in the bigfoot mystery in the Pacific Northwest where he lived. He spent endless hours exploring the Blue Mountains region of Washington with his camcorder. After years of discovering and casting extraordinary foot prints, Paul spotted the golden goose. Steady as a rock, overweight and winded, our man got every second of his bigfoot sighting on film.

Then, he suffered the slings and arrows of humiliation as his video was dismissed by skeptics. He was accused of being a hoaxer. Paul kept returning to the location, hoping to recapture the moment and defend his verity. He failed to duplicate one of the rarest events that can be captured on film, a feat he had already accomplished!

The Freeman film, it's real.

Watch the whole raw footage (about 5 minutes long, not the short clips) and listen as Paul aims the camcorder and does the narration as a huge figure moves across his field of vision, in and out of focus and in and out of sight. Pick up the nuances of height and movement. It's clear Paul is startled by what he is seeing through his viewfinder but he continues to operate the camera through it all.

In wartime, action such this would have earned the guy a medal.

SIGHTING THIRTY-THREE

Foot Prints

MISSION STATEMENT: My name is Barry. I am a Sasquatch. In late June my cousin Dave and I scared a couple of campers near Seneca Rocks, West Virginia. In their haste to leave, one of the campers dropped his smart phone and I found it. As long as the camper allows his phone account to remain active, my blog to explain bigfoot sightings will continue.

Update: The camper read my first post and has agreed to continue funding his smart phone. Thank you Camper One!

BIGFOOT SIGHTINGS EXPLAINED

Foot prints, real or hoax?

See Jeff Meldrum, (*Sasquatch: Science Meets Legend*)

Dr. Meldrum has examined and verified enough forensic foot print evidence of the existence of a Sasquatch to send the likes of the Unabomber, Ted Bundy or the Boston Strangler straight to the electric chair, if any of them were a bigfoot.

SIGHTING THIRTY-FOUR

Campers experience strange events in Brush Mountain Wilderness Area (Virginia)

MISSION STATEMENT: My name is Barry. I am a Sasquatch. In late June my cousin Dave and I scared a couple of campers near Seneca Rocks, West Virginia. In their haste to leave, one of the campers dropped his smart phone and I found it. As long as the camper allows his phone account to remain active, my blog to explain bigfoot sightings will continue.

Update: The camper read my first post and has agreed to continue funding his smart phone. Thank you Camper One!

BIGFOOT SIGHTINGS EXPLAINED

Here is a report* from several campers:

My friends and I were camping in a wilderness area. We experienced knocks and rock throwing. The thing that made us a bit unnerved was that night, in spite of our loud talking, a deer decided to wander up to the camp within about 10 feet and stayed next to us the entire night! This area is frequented by a large numbers of hunters which should have made the deer stay very far away. We also had a large campfire. It seems to me that the deer was seeking a safe place to be because there was obviously something to worry about than us humans. There were several more rocks thrown that night.

TIME AND CONDITIONS: Day and night. Lots of sunlight during the day. The area is a narrow valley surrounded by mountains. There was a brook with a pristine population of Brook Trout. Night was very dark. No moonlight. The temp was warm and the air was very still.

Here is the report* filed by an investigator after speaking to the eyewitness:

The incident started about 3 p.m. after his group of three finished setting up camp

They heard three knocks that sounded like a board being hit against a tree on top of the ridge to their northeast. The three wondered aloud what the sound was but dismissed it as nothing.

About 15 minutes later they heard what sounded to them like small rocks being thrown. They distinguished the sound from falling branches due to the velocity of the object. Rather than a single thud, the objects would hit and then roll through the leaves. Several of these objects hit the tent closest to the ridge line.

The deer that entered their camp arrived about 9 p.m., stayed within 10 feet of the witnesses the entire night and was still there when they woke in the morning. They felt this was very unusual behavior for a wild deer and noticed it would occasionally look off into the woods as though it was alerted to something in the darkness.

The behavior of the deer alone does not suggest the presence of a Sasquatch but wood knocks and rock throws are characteristic of harassment behavior. The witness felt the behavior of the deer, after the knocks and rock throws, was worth including in his report.

Campsite is very heavily forested and full resources a large animal would need to survive and stay concealed.

Here is what really happened:

After setting up camp, the witnesses hear knocks and a few rocks bounce into their camp.

Several hours later a deer walks into the camp and more rocks land in their vicinity. The deer stays the night.

The bigfoot thought this behavior was highly unusual. 99 out of 100 campers cannot pack up and leave fast enough after a second rock is tossed at them.

Some people miss the obvious. The deer didn't.

*The BFRO.net website is the source for material used in this report. The report that appears here has been edited by Barry Bigfoot to conform with proper written English and the known facts.

SIGHTING THIRTY-FIVE

Loch Ness Monster (Scottish Highlands)

MISSION STATEMENT: My name is Barry. I am a Sasquatch. In late June my cousin Dave and I scared a couple of campers near Seneca Rocks, West Virginia. In their haste to leave, one of the campers dropped his smart phone and I found it. As long as the camper allows his phone account to remain active, my blog to explain bigfoot sightings will continue.

Update: The camper read my first post and has agreed to continue funding his smart phone. Thank you Camper One!

Loch Ness Monster

Here is what really happened:

Nothing. Not there. Wishful thinking. Figment of imagination. Light reflecting off a deep, 23 mile freshwater lake. Get over it.

SIGHTING THIRTY-SIX

Late night sighting by motorists on Hwy 60 near the Rockbridge County border (Virginia)

MISSION STATEMENT: My name is Barry. I am a Sasquatch. In late June my cousin Dave and I scared a couple of campers near Seneca Rocks, West Virginia. In their haste to leave, one of the campers dropped his smart phone and I found it. As long as the camper allows his phone account to remain active, my blog to explain bigfoot sightings will continue.

Update: The camper read my first post and has agreed to continue funding his smart phone. Thank you Camper One!

BIGFOOT SIGHTINGS EXPLAINED

Here is a report* from a driver returning from Christmas shopping late at night:

My ex-wife and I were driving on Highway 60 in Rockbridge County, VA about 3-4 miles from the county line. We were returning from Christmas shopping in West Virginia. It was around midnight. I was driving and she was in the passenger seat talking away as usual, when all of a sudden we came upon something standing upright in a field off to the left.

I slowed to a stop and asked my ex "what the hell is that?" She couldn't say a word. We observed the thing from the side of the road. I am a deer hunter and used a spotlight to help illuminate the thing and it was at least 8 foot tall and had to top 500 lbs.

We never talked about this to anyone for fear of being called crazy. This is the first time I have ever breathed a word about it.

I didn't get out of the car or return the next day. As far as i know, this is private property.

The ex-wife, as far as i know, has never and will not speak about it.

Sighting occurred around midnight on a moonless extremely cold Virginia mountain night. Open field, few trees, hillside 25-30 yards from the highway.

Here is the report* filed by an investigator after speaking to the eyewitness:

The witness describes sighting a creature over eight feet tall and very heavy. The creature stood only about 80 feet away and was illuminated by a hand held spotlight.

He described the face as between dark gray and black, with the body covered in rust colored hair. The hair was long and unkempt but not matted. When first sighted, the creature was standing by a four-strand, barbed wire fence. He reported the height was about 3½ feet taller than the fence.

The creature shielded its eyes, attempting to see what the witness was doing. It turned and walked 3 – 4 steps and repeated the attempt to watch the witness. It looked back at the witness periodically during its walk to the treeline.

The witness is relieved to be able to share his experience.

He said his ex-wife doesn't want to discuss the incident.

Here is what really happened:

She was in the passenger seat, talking away as usual.

Now his ex-wife doesn't want to discuss the incident.

She'll take the house and the child support, there is no question about that, but what the hell does she care about his mental health?

Rest assured Mr. Ex, on that cold December eve, your spotlight was pointed at Sebastian, who was on his way home from last minute Christmas shoplifting.

*The BFRO.net website is the source for material used in this report. The report that appears here has been edited by Barry Bigfoot to conform with proper written English and the known facts.

SIGHTING THIRTY-SEVEN

Two Georgia police officers witness a road crossing which is also captured on their Dashcam (Georgia)

MISSION STATEMENT: My name is Barry. I am a Sasquatch. In late June my cousin Dave and I scared a couple of campers near Seneca Rocks, West

Virginia. In their haste to leave, one of the campers dropped his smart phone and I found it. As long as the camper allows his phone account to remain active, my blog to explain bigfoot sightings will continue.

Update: The camper read my first post and has agreed to continue funding his smart phone. Thank you Camper One!

BIGFOOT SIGHTINGS EXPLAINED

Watch the video. Listen carefully to the audio. Decide for yourself if these two officers are great actors (no chance), liars (the audio/video is being recorded inside their vehicle while they are on duty) or completely bewildered when something on two legs runs into the path of their speeding police cruiser.

Georgia Police Bigfoot Road Crossing Facebook Find Bigfoot #47

SIGHTING THIRTY-EIGHT

Driver sees a runner charge at his car near Mt. Solon (Virginia)

MISSION STATEMENT: My name is Barry. I am a Sasquatch. In late June my cousin Dave and I scared a couple of campers near Seneca Rocks, West Virginia. In their haste to leave, one of the campers dropped his smart phone and I found it. As long as the camper allows his phone account to remain active, my blog to explain bigfoot sightings will continue.

Update: The camper read my first post and has agreed to continue funding his smart phone. Thank you Camper One!

BIGFOOT SIGHTINGS EXPLAINED

Here is a report* from a driver who saw a bigfoot at the side of the road.

This was so unreal. The area has a lot of real wilderness throughout and nearby marshes, creeks and deep woods. The incident was about 9:30 pm, Fri. June 2nd. We had been to the theater, grabbed some food and were headed home. Driving north my wife and I saw something rushing along the edge of the road. I said to my wife, "did you see that deer?" She said, "that was no deer!!!"

It was a silvery-white, tall, vertical, slender thing with what she called "flowing" hair.

Our "sighting" was about 3 seconds. This would have been utterly dimissed as something unexplainable, except we went back there the next morning, walked up to a cleared area with some very soft, muddy places. My wife got some poison ivy for her efforts. We found quite a few tracks. There were distinct toe markings. The foot had a "human" look to the shape. This area is teeming with deer, beaver, raccoons, etc. The whole thing is just unreal. You don't expect to see this within sight of a freakin' Walmart.

Almost totally dark, cloudy, had rained earlier

Here is the report* filed by an investigator after speaking to the eyewitness:

This road used to be known for high numbers of road kill, particularly deer and the witness recounts seeing 40-50 deer kills in this section. This night he had his brights on and was travelling approximately 25 mph while watching for deer.

He initially saw something out of the corner of his eye and assumed it was a deer, until he looked over to see a bipedal figure in a running motion. The figure was slightly ahead of the car on the passenger side, running at him. It made an immediate turn away (toward the east) into the dense woods when it was approximately even with the car. At this point he estimated the distance from the car to the figure was fifteen feet. The "flowing hair" noticed by his wife was from the arms as they were moving in a running motion. The hair color seemed to have lighter patches, like highlights. He was unable to see feet or make out facial features or skin color. To him the figure was not "bulky," but more "athletic." He estimated its height to be seven feet.

He was particularly struck by how fast and graceful the figure was, especially since it was moving through patches of thicker brush along the roadside.

Upon return to the area during daylight, he noticed tracks, mostly in clear-cut area with clay soil. The tracks were varying sizes as mentioned, and on several tracks he could easily distinguish toes. His cell phone at the time did not have a camera, and he regrets not being able to take a picture of the tracks. Rain shortly after this precluded a return visit to the site with a camera, as he thought the tracks would likely have been washed away.

I found him to be a credible witness.

Here is what really happened:

The witness saw the figure for only three seconds but he wasn't the only person to see her that night.

A week before this incident happened, Brenda found an exquisite diamond engagement ring at the edge of a distant campsite. A bigfoot has no pockets, of course, so she kept her treasure tightly squeezed inside her huge mitts.

On that dark and windswept night, Brenda dropped the ring. She searched the ground desperately. It was hard to see anything.

Whenever a car came down the road, Brenda ran up to the passenger side and searched in the light.

On one of her runs, our witness rolled by.

A few moments later, another driver, as surprised by her sudden appearance as the previous one, turned his car around to investigate. He flicked on his high beams and Brenda meekly stepped out of the bushes. She scoured the ground for a few seconds, picked up a shiny object, gave a toothy smile to the driver and walked back into the wilderness.

*The BFRO.net website is the source for material used in this report. The report that appears here has been edited by Barry Bigfoot to conform with proper written English and the known facts.

SIGHTING THIRTY-NINE

Survivorman relates his bigfoot encounter on Discovery Channel

MISSION STATEMENT: My name is Barry. I am a Sasquatch. In late June my cousin Dave and I scared a couple of campers near Seneca Rocks, West Virginia. In their haste to leave, one of the campers dropped his smart phone and I found it. As long as the camper allows his phone account to remain active, my blog to explain bigfoot sightings will continue.

Update: The camper read my first post and has agreed to continue funding his smart phone. Thank you Camper One!

BIGFOOT SIGHTINGS EXPLAINED

Les Stroud, Discovery Channel's Survivorman, talks freely about his encounter.

Les was camping in a remote location when he heard bipedal footsteps approach his tent. He listened as whatever it was passed his location and crashed away through the brush. The steps he heard were unlike any animal footfall he had ever experienced in the wild. That the perpetrator could be another person was out of the question. He could muster no explanation.

Here is what really happened:

Yep, Survivorman can go into the most remote places without food, water, shelter or tools and survive there for a good period of time. His chances of encountering one of us are much better than yours are.

Would you like to increase your chances of an encounter?

For a personalized list of remote and vetted sighting locations in your state (excluding Hawaii, Nevada and the District of Columbia), send $3 dollars (no checks) to help cover postage and handling to:

Barry Bigfoot, PO Box 45, Falling Waters, West Virginia 25419-0045.

SIGHTING FORTY

Sighting at sunrise while walking a dog outside of Hightown (Virginia)

MISSION STATEMENT: My name is Barry. I am a Sasquatch. In late June my cousin Dave and I scared a couple of campers near Seneca Rocks, West Virginia. In their haste to leave, one of the campers dropped his smart phone and I found it. As long as the camper allows his phone account to remain active, my blog to explain bigfoot sightings will continue.

Update: The camper read my first post and has agreed to continue funding his smart phone. Thank you Camper One!

BIGFOOT SIGHTINGS EXPLAINED

Here is a report* from a woman walking a dog at sunrise.

This sighting took place in a sparsely populated county of Virginia. It was very early and I was walking one of my sister's dogs. It had been raining but wasn't at the time we were walking. We rounded a corner & saw a figure on the road in front of us crossing the road – maybe about 200 feet away. It was about 5 feet tall (I'm 6 ft. tall & it was a good bit shorter than me). It was on 2 feet, had dark hair all over its body. The arms seemed very long. I could not see the face clearly – it did turn towards us. The arms moved as it walked. I saw it step on the road then across a small ditch & low bank in one stride. It went off into the woods. The dog stood very still & rigid as we watched this figure. He never barked (which was amazing because he barks at everything!). Once the figure disappeared, he wanted to go after it, but of course I turned him around & we walked back to my sister's house.

The next day I checked for footprints. The forest where this figure entered has a "path" seemingly cleared. There is a slight hill & a dip with a creek running through. Just beyond this creek is where the figure crossed the road & up into the woods.

It was overcast, it had rained, but wasn't when the dog & I were walking. It happened between 5:45 & 6 am

This is a mountainous area. Forests & open fields. Lots of deer & other wildlife (i.e. bear, coyote). The entire county is mountains & valleys.

The only other witness is the dog but he's not talkin'!!

Here is the report* filed by an investigator after speaking to the eyewitness:

The bi-pedal figure was already in the road walking from the first moment she saw it.

Its arms were in motion, swinging as it walked, and this prevented her from getting a clear estimate of their length in relationship to the knees, but she had a clear sense that they were longer than normal.

At her distance she couldn't estimate the hair length, but she could tell that it covered the entire body. She is a tall person herself and she knew for sure that the hairy figure was shorter than her. If this was a Sasquatch it was most likely a young one.

As she watched, it exited to the right side of the road and walked into the woods, uphill and away from the valley bottom.

The witness estimates a full minute transpired from the time she first first noticed the figure to the point it disappeared into the trees.

Here is what really happened:

You can't really blame Teddy for this one.

The witness was visiting her sister and had gotten up early to walk the family dog. Teddy had crossed there before but the homeowner had never gotten up this early. The witness even found evidence of his path.

Teddy is almost 10 years old and he is a little over five feet tall. He did exactly as he was supposed to do. He continued across the road and quickly jumped the ditch, but he twisted his ankle when he landed. That is why he remembers this sighting so well. It took him one slow and painful minute to reach the tree line and disappear into the woods. He thanks the witness for restraining her dog.

*The BFRO.net website is the source for material used in this report. The report that appears here has been edited by Barry Bigfoot to conform with proper written English and the known facts.

SIGHTING FORTY-ONE

Unidentified animal spotted this week – The Southwest Times (Virginia)

MISSION STATEMENT: My name is Barry. I am a Sasquatch. In late June my cousin Dave and I scared a couple of campers near Seneca Rocks, West Virginia. In their haste to leave, one of the campers dropped his smart

phone and I found it. As long as the camper allows his phone account to remain active, my blog to explain bigfoot sightings will continue.

Update: The camper read my first post and has agreed to continue funding his smart phone. Thank you Camper One!

BIGFOOT SIGHTINGS EXPLAINED

Monday, September 09, 2013

By Roger Williams
The Southwest Times

Unidentified animal spotted this week

This eyewitness account was provided by Leroy Early of the Robinson Tract Community. He says he was taking his dog out, just at dusk Wednesday night, about 8:30 – 9 p.m., when he noticed a large furry animal standing in his backyard. He heard a rasping noise similar to a guttural grunt from the edge of the yard near the tree-line that attracted his attention ... he looked up and saw an animal standing upright that he estimated to be between six and seven feet tall. The animal was covered in thick fur and apparently was investigating his chicken coop or the chicken feeder near the coop. His little dog scampered back toward the house in a whimpering, tail-between-her-legs rush, after scenting this unknown animal. He made haste to join her in the relative safety of his home and made sure his shotgun was nearby. He said it then ran quickly into the woods and out of sight, still on two legs. Later that evening he and his wife heard what sounded like a thump in the trees close to his backyard. He insists this is a true account of what he observed that night. He stated that he would not have called to report the sighting had it not been for the picture published in The Southwest Times Aug. 26. If there are other witnesses who have seen the strange animal roaming the mountains of this area, do not hesitate to pass this information on.
Written by: Editor on September 9, 2013.

Here is what really happened:

This article is straightforward, unbiased and all of the facts are correct.

Except one.

Jay was not "apparently" investigating the chicken coop.

He'd already figured out the latch.

The Southwest Times "Serving Virginia Since 1906" southwesttimes.com.

SIGHTING FORTY-TWO

Michael D. Greene's "Squeaky" is caught on thermal video in the act of swiping gifts (North Carolina)

MISSION STATEMENT: My name is Barry. I am a Sasquatch. In late June my cousin Dave and I scared a couple of campers near Seneca Rocks, West Virginia. In their haste to leave, one of the campers dropped his smart phone and I found it. As long as the camper allows his phone account to remain active, my blog to explain bigfoot sightings will continue.

Update: The camper read my first post and has agreed to continue funding his smart phone. Thank you Camper One!

BIGFOOT SIGHTINGS EXPLAINED

Here is what really happened:

This is real.

Pay Michael the $2 to download the video or find it for free somewhere on the internet. Watch it a few dozen times in amazement and try and convince yourself you're seeing a man in a costume. I'm not surprised Michael Greene fooled "Squeaky" by hiding his thermal image camera and leaving it running while he drove away for a few hours.

"Squeaky", who is better known as Big Tony, enjoyed all of the treats. You can see his reaction after he retreats into the trees. He stands there for a long time rocking back and forth, licking his lips after eating the Snickers, looking back longingly at the stump where he'd bent down and picked up the candy and wishing another Mars bar might magically appear on the stump before reluctantly backing away and walking off camera.

A thermal camera forms an image using infrared radiation. All objects (including bodies, human or animal) emit a certain amount of radiation as a function of their temperatures.

A thermal camera reveals the full figure of a body and all of it's parts. The body appears as a white image moving against a dark background.

The creature in this video has a pointed head, no neck, massive shoulders, an enormous chest and very long arms. A man? A man in a costume?

Look for yourself.

See Michael D.Greene, Bigfoot thermal video, North Carolina.

Report by Native Americans at Ft. Coville (Washington State)

MISSION STATEMENT: My name is Barry. I am a Sasquatch. In late June my cousin Dave and I scared a couple of campers near Seneca Rocks, West Virginia. In their haste to leave, one of the campers dropped his smart phone and I found it. As long as the camper allows his phone account to remain active, my blog to explain bigfoot sightings will continue.

Update: The camper read my first post and has agreed to continue funding his smart phone. Thank you Camper One!

BIGFOOT SIGHTINGS EXPLAINED

Here are highlights from a report* given by Native Americans to the Rev. Elkanah Walker at Ft. Coville, Washington.

"They hunt and do their work at night...They belong to a race of giants which inhabit a certain mountain off to the west of us...They say their track is about a foot and a half long. They will carry two beams upon their back at once...they frequently come in the night, steal salmon from the nets, and eat them raw. If the people are away they always know when they are coming very near by their strong smell, which is most intolerable. It is not uncommon for them to come in the night and give three whistles. Then the stones will begin to hit the houses. The people are troubled by their nocturnal visits"

Here is what really happened:

This report could have been written in Washington State today.

It was not.

It was written in 1840.

Fort Coville, a territorial army post built to monitor the border and prevent trouble between the settlers and the Indians, closed in 1882.

Descendants of the bigfoots in this report still inhabit the area and still stink up the place.

*Meldrum, J., *Sasquatch Legend Meets Science*, pp 85-6.

Daytime sighting near the Virginia Motor Speedway given in great detail (Virginia)

MISSION STATEMENT: My name is Barry. I am a Sasquatch. In late June my cousin Dave and I scared a couple of campers near Seneca Rocks, West Virginia. In their haste to leave, one of the campers dropped his smart phone and I found it. As long as the camper allows his phone account to remain active, my blog to explain bigfoot sightings will continue.

Update: The camper read my first post and has agreed to continue funding his smart phone. Thank you Camper One!

BIGFOOT SIGHTINGS EXPLAINED

Here is a report* from a driver who was shaken up by what he saw.

This incident has been bothering me for a long time.

The sighting occurred just north of a crest in the road, where you could not see the trough until you had actually gotten on top of the crest.The sighting took place on the downside of the hill, almost towards the bottom.

My girlfriend and I were driving back from Norfolk to Maryland on Route 17. As I was driving over one hill, I noticed a dead animal in the road on the slower lane ahead. It appeared to be a large dead dog.

As I approached, I had to change lanes and started to notice a smell that reminded me of muck we use to pull out of the creek near where I grew up. The odor got stronger and I thought it was an unusual smell for a dead animal, which now appeared to be the size and color of a german shephard.

As I drove around the animal, I watched so I would not accidentally hit it as I went by (it straddled the lane markers a bit). I also noticed what I thought was a little old black man crouching in the woods behind a leafy branch, waiting for me to pass by.

My immediate thought was that he was coming out to get his poor dog that got run over. I watched him in my rear view mirror. What I saw surprised me.

The figure came out of the woods, certainly bigger than I had thought it would have been. But what amazed me was that it reached the middle of the road in three strides. It looked down at the dead animal just as another car was coming over the crest behind me.

It stood in a crouch, with its hands well below its knees, sort of in a monkey like position. It appeared startled as it jerked its head looking towards the oncoming car, I saw what looked like two long furry ears (possibly dread-lock type hair) swing around, following its head. My first impression was that it looked like one of those old aviator hats with the long "ear pieces" but with hair.

As soon as it was startled by the other car, it turned and took another two and a half steps back into the woods. What amazed me was the length of the stride.

I started to to get physically shaken.

We stopped a few minutes later at a roadside store to soothe my nerves. That's when I realized that I might have seen an animal and not a man. To this day, I cannot tell you exactly what I saw. But it was definitely NOT what I originally thought it was.

Just moments before dusk. Clear day, typical hot-sticky weather for Virginia in August, clouds covering the sun.

Here is the report* filed by an investigator after speaking to the eyewitness:

The witness added:

I had told my kids about the "encounter" and always made great pains not to embellish the story, and to leave the decision of what I saw up to the imagination of the listener. I did make it a point to not mention what I thought it was. I always said, "I don't know what exactly it was I saw, but I can tell you what happened. You decide."

Please remember that my focus was on avoiding hitting the road kill and that my eyes were definitely diverted away from the road in front of me for a split second.

It was in this split second that this figure caught my attention, enough to look back in my rear view mirror. As I passed it, I did not catch any facial features, only that it had a dark complexion (not Caucasian).

I wondered why someone would be just inside the edge of the woods as most of us would be just OUTSIDE the edge of the woods if we were waiting to get a peek at something in the road.

I was given the distinct, split second impression that he/it was hiding at the edge of the woods, waiting for me to go by. I cannot explain what gave me that impression.

I do remember thinking that this subject was bigger than I had instinctively thought. And what really did catch my attention was the size of its gait. The impression I had out of the corner of my eye was that, whatever or whomever it was was in a squatting position. I would say that I had the impression that it was bigger than I was at the time (I was 6'3" and about 225 then).

It briefly stood hunched over the road kill, with its fingertips cupped, extending slightly below the knees, in a stance unlike us normal humans. The knees were bent slightly.

I remember wondering how in the world whatever I saw could only have taken such few steps to get back to the edge of the woods. It was this thought that shook me up.

The only thing that was noticeable was the swamp like stench that permeated the area. I do not remember the smell lingering after I had passed the area in question.

I am making no claims as to the exact identity of the subject.

For all I know, it could have been a big black guy, wearing a hairy aviator cap, who could run at a fast pace with huge strides and who didn't have the best posture in the world.

Here is what really happened:

The witness is observant. He is detail oriented and self-effacing. What he saw off to his right and again in his rear view mirror was Junior, who was determined to retrieve the dead animal before a rival bigfoot could get to it first.

Route 17 is a busy six lane highway and Crazy Stanley was crouching on the opposite side of the road. Stanley had his eyes on the road kill as well, but Junior got there first. Big man that he is, Junior shared his prize with Stanley. How much dog can anyone eat in just one sitting anyway?

*The BFRO.net website is the source for material used in this report. The report that appears here has been edited by Barry Bigfoot to conform with proper written English and the known facts.

SIGHTING FORTY-FIVE

Patterson-Gimlin, the No. 1 most famous bigfoot video, Bluff Creek (California)

MISSION STATEMENT: My name is Barry. I am a Sasquatch. In late June my cousin Dave and I scared a couple of campers near Seneca Rocks, West Virginia. In their haste to leave, one of the campers dropped his smart phone and I found it. As long as the camper allows his phone account to remain active, my blog to explain bigfoot sightings will continue.

Update: The camper read my first post and has agreed to continue funding his smart phone. Thank you Camper One!

BIGFOOT SIGHTINGS EXPLAINED

Patterson-Gimlin film, Bluff Creek, California

Here is what really happened:

The very first instance of a bigfoot caught on film was truly worthy of further scientific study when it was released in 1967. The footage had our community pretty shaken as well.

However, skeptics and hoaxers quickly smothered the film with misinformation and criticism and the topic quickly returned to the loony files with the UFO's.

The film is real.

Everything is real — their reasons for riding deep into the forest to document their search, their behavior when they spot "Patty", her size, her muscles, the shine of her coat, the light-colored pads on the soles of her huge feet, her long stride, her ample breasts bouncing in the sunlight, the swollen bruise on her right thigh**, her turn and peek back at the cowboys, the footprints she left in the sand as she hurried into the woods and Bob Gimlin's calm insistence for almost fifty years (Roger Patterson died in 1972) that the encounter happened just as it played out in front of them and in front of the camera.

Patterson. Gimlin. Patty. Two real American heroes and one frightened female bigfoot.

**1967-era Hollywood costumers were not capable of creating such a dynamic, moving figure, let alone two cowboys who were trying to film a documentary with a rented camera.

SIGHTING FORTY-SIX

Daniel Boone – Pioneer, Woodsman, Explorer, 1734 – 1820 (Kentucky)

MISSION STATEMENT: My name is Barry. I am a Sasquatch. In late June my cousin Dave and I scared a couple of campers near Seneca Rocks, West Virginia. In their haste to leave, one of the campers dropped his smart phone and I found it. As long as the camper allows his phone account to remain active, my blog to explain bigfoot sightings will continue.

Update: The camper read my first post and has agreed to continue funding his smart phone. Thank you Camper One!

BIGFOOT SIGHTINGS EXPLAINED

Daniel Boone, "the "rippin'est, roarin'est, fightin'est man the frontier ever knew."

This schmuck shot first and never bothered to ask questions.

Daniel Boone told tales of "killing a ten-foot, hairy giant he called a Yahoo," says John Mack Faragher in a 1992 biography of Boone.

We called him old 'Trigger Finger' even though he had pour powder into the rifle and load a musket ball before he could fire a shot.

Daniel Boone never killed any of us.

If he had killed one of us, he never would have made it to Kentucky, let alone another ten yards.

SIGHTING FORTY-SEVEN

Clear Image Bigfoot Captured on Game Camera at Greenbrier Sporting Club in White Sulphur Springs (West Virginia)

MISSION STATEMENT: My name is Barry. I am a Sasquatch. In late June my cousin Dave and I scared a couple of campers near Seneca Rocks, West Virginia. In their haste to leave, one of the campers dropped his smart phone and I found it. As long as the camper allows his phone account to remain active, my blog to explain bigfoot sightings will continue.

Update: The camper read my first post and has agreed to continue funding his smart phone. Thank you Camper One!

BIGFOOT SIGHTINGS EXPLAINED

Clear Image Bigfoot Captured on Game Camera at Greenbrier Sporting Club

Here is what really happened:

Nobody's life should be summed up in a Candid Camera moment.

He was nearly blind, stooped, tired and very close to the end. Harvey (now deceased) is the bigfoot who's still image was captured by the Greenbrier Sporting Club's game trail camera. The photo and accompanying video can be seen on YouTube.

He was digging for termites in the stump. He just couldn't hunt any more. His mind was not on human gadgets. Who needs a game trail camera anyway?

Harvey was an honorable father and a good provider but his memory is forever besmirched by a breach of protocol (being caught on film) and a YouTube video which mocks his very existence.

Watch it for yourself.

Go to YouTube and type in:

Clear Image Bigfoot Captured on Game Camera at Greenbrier Sporting Club

Where's the body?

MISSION STATEMENT: My name is Barry. I am a Sasquatch. In late June my cousin Dave and I scared a couple of campers near Seneca Rocks, West Virginia. In their haste to leave, one of the campers dropped his smart phone and I found it. As long as the camper allows his phone account to remain active, my blog to explain bigfoot sightings will continue.

Update: The camper read my first post and has agreed to continue funding his smart phone. Thank you Camper One!

BIGFOOT SIGHTINGS EXPLAINED

Most asked questions:

Q. Why hasn't anyone found a body? Where is the fossil evidence?

A. After one of us passes, we hold a dignified ceremony and then we eat him. We're talking about hundreds of pounds of protein and fat here, and the marrow in the bones, it's yummy.

Don't make a face. You guys did the same thing 20,000 years ago, and that Donner party thing happened in California in 1846, so don't act so superior.

Q. What if a bigfoot passes away all alone?

A. That almost never happens. Scavengers quickly take care of business and what remains can be easily mistaken for any large furry animal. Who is even wondering? What busy citizen is going to call the Department of Natural Resources or take us to a lab somewhere to verify anything?

Q. Still, what are the chances of finding a dead Sasquatch?

A. I e-mailed the bookmakers at the MGM Grand in Las Vegas. Their response was, "The odds of finding a dead Sasquatch are the same as finding the tooth fairy or the Easter Bunny, but bring in the body".

JFK Assassination Conspiracy (Texas)

MISSION STATEMENT: My name is Barry. I am a Sasquatch. In late June my cousin Dave and I scared a couple of campers near Seneca Rocks, West Virginia. In their haste to leave, one of the campers dropped his smart phone and I found it. As long as the camper allows his phone account to remain active, my blog to explain bigfoot sightings will continue.

Update: The camper read my first post and has agreed to continue funding his smart phone. Thank you Camper One!

The John F. Kennedy Assassination Conspiracy 1963

Vice-president Lyndon B. Johnson (cover-up), the elder George Bush (operations and cover-up), FBI Director J. Edgar Hoover (cover-up), top criminals and their henchmen (operations and cover-up), CIA operatives (operations and cover-up), Lee Harvey Oswald (the fall guy, served up on a silver platter by the CIA and silenced only hours after insisting to the press that he was being set up), Jack Ruby (cover-up), elected Dallas officials (operations), wealthy Texans (finance), ex-CIA Chief Allen Dulles (cover-up), senator Gerald R. Ford (cover-up), compounded by a compromised Secret Service, a corrupt Dallas Police Department and the journalists of yesterday who were bamboozled by a manufactured avalanche of lies and nonsense.

How do I know this?

Cousin Earnest was there in Dealey Plaza on Nov. 22. 1963. He was on the grassy knoll, hiding in a tree above the picket fence. Earnest had overheard a radio broadcast announcing the President and Mrs. Kennedy were coming to Dallas. He was a big fan. He got there early (4 a.m.) and waited for the motorcade (noon).

Before the Presidential motorcade turned onto Elm Street, Earnest saw two men standing a short distance from where he was hiding. He assumed they were police or secret service until the smaller of the two opened fire with his kill shot.

The two men packed up in an instant and walked calmly through the frantic crowd as people raced up the hill towards the fence. No one looked in the trees.

Dealey Plaza was now a crime scene and Earnest was stuck there for hours until he could retreat to the railroad tracks.

Now that Earnest knew the murder was a conspiracy, it wasn't hard to put the pieces together. He can talk about it for hours.

SIGHTING FIFTY

UFO's

MISSION STATEMENT: My name is Barry. I am a Sasquatch. In late June my cousin Dave and I scared a couple of campers near Seneca Rocks, West Virginia. In their haste to leave, one of the campers dropped his smart phone and I found it. As long as the camper allows his phone account to remain active, my blog to explain bigfoot sightings will continue.

Update: The camper read my first post and has agreed to continue funding his smart phone. Thank you Camper One!

ALIENS

These guys have had no interest in us since your hominid family split from our family 4.2 million years ago.

At Australopithecus anamensis on the evolutionary tree, you went your way and we went ours.

The aliens want you. For what reason or purpose, I do not know.

The terrifying abductions, the mutilating of cattle, the crop fields carved into unfathomable designs, the hide and seek games with jet fighter pilots, the slow passes over Intercontinental Ballistic Missile Silos? That's your problem.

They don't care if we see them. We see them fly their space ships straight into the lake and stay there. We see this happen a lot.

Talk about wasting your good time, imagine if you're a bigfoot with a smart phone and you want to report to the Boone County Sheriff's Department that right now, at this very moment, a UFO is sitting at the bottom of Plum Orchard Lake?

About the author

Barry Bigfoot

Age, height, weight, color, marital status, health, religion, service, hobbies and awards cannot be divulged for reasons of security. Needless to say, Barry is a member of an endangered species that does not exist.

Education:

Home schooling through age 16

Higher Education: If you consider how resourceful he was during the four years he prowled the grounds of Shepherd College in Shepherdstown, West Virginia, Barry merits a four year degree. He found texts in dumpsters; collected discarded magazines, newspapers, term papers, documents and doctoral studies; audited classes (especially evening classes) from up in the trees; evesdropped on dorms; poked around labs and buildings at night and tracked study groups in the field. He majored in philosophy with minors in physics and history.

Graduate Work:

Masters in Field Training Arts (MFTA)

Current Residence:

West Virginia

This is his first publication.

Contact Information

Barry Bigfoot. PO Box 45, Falling Waters, West Virginia 25419-0045

Report your sighting to Barry and receive Barry's analysis. Write down everything you can remember, send your report, include your return address and $3 (no checks) for processing and handling and receive Barry's take on your unique experience.

For a personalized list of vetted and remote sighting locations near you (excluding Hawaii, Nevada and the District of Columbia) send $3 (no checks) for processing and handling, Include your return address.

Ask Barry. Ask Barry about anything! Whether your question pertains to science, history, health, religion, politics, social issues, sports or life, ask Barry. Mail your question and $3 (no checks) for processing and handling to Post Office Box 45, Falling Waters, West Virginia 25419-0045. Include your return address.

www.ingramcontent.com/pod-product-compliance
Lightning Source LLC
Chambersburg PA
CBHW070535130626
46555CB00003B/1425